SAVAGE LIES

A HIGH SCHOOL BULLY ROMANCE

HIDDEN VALLEY ELITE
BOOK ONE

ISLA VAUGHN

ARROWSCOPE PRESS, LLC

CHAPTER ONE

RILEY

"*There's always an angle. A vulnerability. Find it and exploit it.*" Words I lived by my entire life. Words handed down from mom and my uncle Ronan. Mom was always five steps ahead of everyone else. I wasn't far behind, but there was room for improvement.

Surrounded by boxes, I stood in the middle of the large space that would be my new bedroom for however long we would be there. The early morning sun sliced through the partially open blinds. Out of all the dumps we'd stayed in, it was decent.

Much better than where we stayed on our last, very short visit to Santa Monica, California. We'd stayed long enough for me to crash a beach party, get caught stealing, then have an incredibly hot guy steal a kiss that shattered my world before all hell broke loose, as usual, and we had to leave in a panic-inducing rush.

I didn't know why we were back a year later. We never went to the same place twice. It was driving me crazy, and Mom was tight-lipped about it, which wasn't normal.

Pain shot through my jaw, and I instinctively relaxed the

clench of my teeth. It was the start of a new day in a town where I would have to go to yet another school. The first day was the worst. I glanced at my clock and groaned. I had an hour to get ready.

Coffee. It was the only way I would survive.

I took half a step toward the door when an aggressive, heavy-handed knock sounded. The hairs on the back of my neck stood at attention. Mom didn't rap with her knuckles like that.

"Open up, kid. I've got donuts."

Uncle Ronan. My shoulders relaxed, and I hurried to the door and curled my fingers around the knob before fully opening it. At the sight of his big frame in the doorway, I scowled, a flash of annoyance ripping through me, despite how good it was to see him.

"What, is it Christmas already?" I propped a hand on my hip and glared. I couldn't remember the last time he'd visited wherever we were.

He snorted. "Same fuck-the-world attitude as my sister." After a glance around the room and at the half-unpacked boxes, he shoved a small white bag in my hands. "Donuts."

I scowled harder, holding out my other hand for the coffee clutched in his mammoth fist. His deep laugh filled the room, and I reluctantly softened… but not until he gave me the drink.

"This isn't my first drive-by, brat. I've dealt with your mom for most of my life." He handed over the coffee. "I know how to soothe the beast." He buried his hand in the rat's nest on my head then pulled me in for a hug.

It lasted longer than usual, and I snorted at the reason why. "Your hand's stuck, isn't it?"

I set the bag down on one of the boxes I hadn't opened yet and helped him untangle himself from my long and messy hair. *Why is he here?* I needed to talk to Mom. She was one of the most strategic, intelligent, and cunning people I knew, and I

couldn't help but think she called him, the only other family I was allowed to associate with, to check on me for a reason. My grandparents and the sperm donor, as my mom referred to my father, were off-limits.

I chugged more than half the coffee then felt capable of facing whatever this was with my uncle. "Why are you here?"

Dark eyebrows rose. "Is that all you have to say after I brought you breakfast?"

I dropped onto my bed, shoved back farther so my back was against the headboard, then crossed my legs at the ankles and observed him. His dark-brown hair, the same shade as mine and Mom's, was longer than usual, and there was more than a five o'clock shadow covering his face. He wore black jeans and a Henley, even though it was the end of summer and hot. Alarm bells blared in my head.

"What's going on?" *Are we on the run?* We often moved to stay ahead of any threats from past cons. *Has one of Mom's marks found us? Or worse—Dad?* "Where's Mom?"

"She's out of town with her boyfriend. You're on your own to get to school for your first day. It's some swanky place that's supposed to help you get into college. It's paid up for the year."

"Her new mark?" I sat straighter, shock rolling through me. She always shared everything with me about her cons, but she hadn't this time. I narrowed my gaze on Uncle Ronan. It made his presence even more suspect. Later, I would deal with the "paid up for the year" comment.

"Not this time. There's no con."

Bullshit. "Why are you here? Just to pay for my education?" That sounded shitty. "And thank you for that." He always made sure I had what I needed when Mom couldn't. But a private high school I didn't need or want.

He nodded then leaned against the doorjamb. "What? I can't visit my favorite niece?"

I was his only niece. "Are you in on this con?" It would

explain the dark clothes and the casual attitude that screamed trouble.

"Stop being so suspicious. I have business nearby. When Raelyn told me where you guys were moving, I thought I would come by. That's it. Nothing else is going on."

"Hm." I didn't believe him for a second. But regardless, I was happy to see him. It'd been too long since his last visit. "Are you sticking around?"

"I gotta take off, kid, but I'll try to swing back in a week or so."

Well, hell. I set my empty to-go cup on the nightstand that came with the rental and swung my legs off the bed. Once I was in front of him, his thick arms wrapped me in a tight hug. *Dammit.* I squeezed him just as hard. I'd missed him too.

When he released me, I stepped back and did another pass over his hands, checking for bruising. There wasn't any, but that didn't mean he'd handled whatever business brought him this way before he stopped by.

"Walk me out," he commanded, but the deep tones held a softness others didn't get.

I followed his six-foot-plus frame toward the back of the furnished house. The rear door was off the kitchen, and Uncle Ronan paused, his gruff expression turning serious. I met his dark-brown eyes, something the three of us shared. It was obvious we were related. He and Mom could've been twins with their chestnut hair and olive skin. While he had the same high cheekbones as Mom, his jaw was square, while her face was more heart-shaped. She was drop-dead gorgeous. Heads turned when she walked past. I was told—by the people who loved me, my uncle and mom—that I looked like a younger copy of her, that I was beautiful. But they had to say that. I owned a mirror. I didn't believe them for a second. Regardless of how similar we all looked, it was risky for us to meet Uncle Ronan in certain places.

We couldn't let dear old Dad know where we were.

It was complicated. But so were our lives.

"How's the car running?"

I had a sweet midnight-blue Dodge Charger souped up to compete in NASCAR if I was into that sort of thing, which he'd given me for my sixteenth birthday.

I couldn't help but grin, pushing through the heaviness of the morning. I loved that car. "Good. No problems."

"Are you keeping up with the oil changes?"

I rolled my eyes. "Yes." He'd made sure I knew everything there was to know about taking care of the car before he'd officially handed over the keys. It had been a great week because he'd spent the entire time with us, even if it was to give me a crash course in mechanics.

"And diving? Are you going to take it up here at the new school?"

"Yes." I smacked one of his overdeveloped biceps. Mom had promised last year that this place would be a fresh start… until it wasn't. But she swore her plan, whatever that was, would work this time. "I'm getting a scholarship to go to any college I want. We both know it." Maybe that was why the new school was set up, but I couldn't help to think there was more to it.

"That's the way to do it, kid." He pinched my chin between his thumb and forefinger, lifting it slightly so our gazes held. "This is a different area than what we're used to, but don't think the people aren't as vicious or manipulative as they are in the rougher neighborhoods. If I need to come back here to knock some heads around, I will. Don't let any boys get into your pretty little head."

I lightly smacked his hand, knocking his hold away. "Like I'd ever let that happen. Do you think I've learned nothing by growing up how I did?"

He grunted then pulled me in for another bone-crushing hug. "Love you, kid. You call me if you need anything."

"Even if I need a body buried?" I was kidding, but I knew he would do it if I asked. What he did for a living was suspect.

"Always."

When the door—the back one that didn't have a Ring doorbell or any other cameras—closed behind him, I shut and locked it then hurried to the shower.

Once dressed and ready, I grabbed a donut before rushing out the door.

None of this was normal.

Mom didn't have boyfriends, at least not real ones, and she always filled me in on the details of her cons. She'd shared some or all of her plans with Uncle Ronan. *Why is she shutting me out?*

After pulling up the address to the high school, my mood went from bad to worse. It was another first day at a new school, but this time, I was going in blind.

CHAPTER TWO

COLE

I tasted her kiss again in my dreams, the girl I couldn't place with the slender neck, big almond-shaped brown eyes... then her lips, soft and full, parting under my insistence. She melted into me when I crowded her against the wall. She fit.

She drove me mad. One taste was never enough.

Then I awoke, like always, without a name or a clear enough grasp of her features to find her. Her soft skin and the way she responded, followed me into the shower, and I rubbed one out to her moan ringing in my ears.

I wanted to yank her from my mind and into my arms for real. Someday, I would find her. But probably not today.

The thud of the front door slamming echoed in the upstairs hallway as I pulled my shirt over my head and left my bedroom. Laughter drifted from the foyer, and I grinned as our cousins' voices traveled toward the kitchen, where I knew our house-keeper, Louisa, was laying out a meal to feed the four of us and Dad if he was around. I doubted he was, because he'd been gone since sometime yesterday.

Today was the start of my senior year, and I knew Louisa would put out an elaborate spread. Our cousins, Phoenix and

Shane, devoured food as quickly as my brother, Damon, and I, especially with football practices in full swing. That they ate with us eased the strain on Aunt Cece's bank account, and ours was their home away from home.

I pounded on Damon's door as I went past. "Get your ass out of bed. We leave in twenty." A muffled groan sounded, followed by a thump as his feet hit the floor. He was out of bed, at least. I slammed my fist on the white-paneled wood once more before heading to the kitchen.

When I rounded the corner, it was to my cousins stuffing their faces at the oversized island and Louisa blushing at Shane's compliments. I cracked him on the back of the head as I went by before grabbing a plate then piling it high with a loaded omelet and fruit.

"Morning." I thanked Louisa with a side hug before she handed me a cup of coffee and a glass of water.

Damon came in halfway dressed, tossed his shirt on an empty seat next to him, and fell onto a chair at the island just as Shane chucked a biscuit at his head. He grinned at Louisa, and they exchanged a few words, ignoring our cousins for a minute. Their relationship was more mother-and-son than the one he'd had with our own mom. She took care of us, and we appreciated the hell out of her even more after losing our mom. That day stayed with us, tainting our every waking hour and fucking us up even more than we already had been.

My phone pinged in my pocket, and I pulled it out, glancing at the screen. It was an alarm to one of Dad's rental properties. I'd thought it was vacant. Weird. I'd have to check on the house after practice.

"Where's Dad?" Damon asked.

Louisa made herself scarce at his question, a frustrated expression pinching her weathered features. She disapproved but would never say anything about our absent father.

"Probably at work already," I said with a grunt, but Damon

and I exchanged a knowing glance. I could bet money the text I'd just gotten was from him. He'd been absent all weekend, no doubt with his flavor of the week. He would leave for work from wherever they were together. My guess was the city. Neither of us cared.

"That was a missed opportunity," Phoenix said while blocking his brother for the last roll. "We could've had a party here to kick off your last year at Hidden Valley Academy."

"Rub it in, dick." Damon swiped the bread out of Phoenix's hand and took a giant bite. "We have another year after Cole goes," he grumbled with his mouth full.

"We'll dominate this year and next." Shane shrugged. "Then be at Thane with him. It'll fly by."

I already had a scholarship to Thane University, and I knew the three of them would be offered one this year, once the Division-I schools were allowed to talk to them. That wasn't the problem. My brother wasn't looking forward to the year of separation until he joined me at Thane. I didn't blame him. I wouldn't want to be stuck here alone with Dad, either, not that he would be around much. But still…

"I'm surprised you're here alone," Damon shot back at Shane, a dark look I knew too well brewing in his eyes. "You're usually attached at the hip to Tracey."

"Knock it off." I had to put a stop to Damon's verbal hit before the two of them were on the floor, exchanging punches. "We gotta leave." Phoenix stood when I did and shoved Shane toward the front door.

Of the four of us, Phoenix and I were most alike, not in looks but in demeanor. The front door closed not even a minute later, and I paused before leaving. "I'll see you at school."

I grabbed my gear for fighting. My football stuff was already at school. If there was time, I wanted to meet the guys in the school's basement after and get in a round or two in the ring before heading home. Based on the tension in the air, Damon and Shane could use an outlet aside from football practice to get out some extra aggression.

As I tossed my bag into the car, my phone buzzed again in my pocket. A glance at the screen showed Dad's photo, and I shoved it back into my pocket. I didn't have time to deal with him.

It rang again. *Seems he had time for me today. Fuck.* I didn't want to deal with him. My fingers clamped around the edge of the case, and I yanked my phone out, hit the accept button, and pressed it to my ear. "What?"

"Is there a problem?"

The sternness in Dad's voice whipped through the speaker, and I ground my teeth. I needed to calm down and deal with him. "I'm in a hurry. Is there anything you need?"

He waited a beat, probably deciding if it was worth reprimanding me about my attitude or just telling me what he wanted so we could get off the phone. "My secretary informs me that you have yet to respond to her email."

This again? "That's because I don't want to intern at your office this summer. There will only be two months after I graduate before I leave for preseason at Thane."

"Assuming that's where you'll—"

"It is. We discussed this. I have a scholarship, and you said you would pay any remaining fees. Is that not the case anymore?" My fingers tightened on my phone, and I forced myself to ease up so it didn't crack. But if he dangled the funds against doing the internship, all bets were off—I would need a new phone.

"We're getting off track. The internship isn't negotiable. It'll look good to the college and will count toward your requirements for your major."

If I went pre-law, he meant, but I wasn't. I refused to be anything like him.

CHAPTER THREE

RILEY

Other kids dealt with abandonment issues, loneliness, teen angst. Not me.

Until now. This feeling, the hole in my heart, was new. I had no one. Mom's boyfriend got her emotional investment. Uncle Ronan was off doing what he did. That left... nobody.

Friends, at least real ones, weren't part of my life. I couldn't text my BFF to complain or meet up somewhere *because Mom had rules*. The sense of betrayal was real. Was she following them? I thought not. Then why should I?

I didn't like being alone with my thoughts when it felt like my safety net was gone. So I did the only thing I could and cranked up the music to got lost in Alanis Morissette's lyrics.

My car purred along the winding roads, and I blasted the music louder, trying to shake my shitty mood. So far, nothing had worked. Aggravation hummed in tandem with the engine, heating my blood.

I was used to being on my own while Mom ran a con until it was my turn to gain additional information or provide the catalyst needed to push the mark into the results we wanted.

But her absence because of a boyfriend? No, that wasn't

normal, and a sense of impending doom hung in the air around me even that high speed and loud music couldn't shake loose.

My GPS showed the school a few blocks ahead. The traffic bottleneck could have told me that as I slowed to a crawl. With the windows down, a warm breeze held hints of coffee and had me turning to scan the shops that lined the street. "There you are." Half a block on my left, I recognized the coffeehouse I'd worked at for all of a few days a year ago. That would be my first stop on most mornings. I had my addiction to feed. A glance at the time on my dash showed I had fifteen minutes to get through traffic, park, and find the social services office to get my schedule and locker. First days were the worst.

The closer I got to the school's parking lot, the more I noticed the types of cars pulling in. Expensive. That fit for an academy, where the tuition had to have been astronomical. We didn't do expensive schools or diving coaches. It was another point of contention for my conversation with Mom tonight.

As I turned in and parked, I scanned the kids milling about. The weather was cool for August in California, more like where our last score had been. Vermont had been a quick grab and dash, since Mom wasn't comfortable there because of the proximity to New York—somewhere she said I could not go under any circumstances. The fear in her eyes had been the only thing that made me heed her warning… well, that and a faded memory of her badly beaten face and body when someone from there had caught up with her. She'd never said who. I had my suspicions.

I glanced at my phone one last time, hoping for a text from her but finding nothing. That was unlike her. We would have words later.

I scanned the fanciest school I'd attended, all dark brick and limestone columns. The windows were framed in the same material as the entryway. The place screamed money. The one good thing was that there wasn't a uniform, and from the looks of it, my tight jeans and cropped graphic tee would fit right in. That was how I liked it. The less I stood out the better.

I parked next to a black Range Rover, one of three in the row, grabbed my backpack from the passenger seat, and got out. After locking my car and shoving the key fob into the front pocket of my jeans, I pulled my long hair, which was my natural shade of chestnut brown for once, to one side and slung my bag over my shoulder. Students congregated everywhere. A medley of music, from hip-hop to rock, filled the air as I walked through the parking lot and toward the school's front doors.

Someone cried out. Tires screeched, and I turned abruptly then slammed into a rock wall. "Goddammit." I stumbled back a half step. A hand grasped my elbow, steadying me.

I mumbled thanks to whoever had kept me upright. Dazed from how my head had been jarred from smacking into what must have been a person and not a brick wall, I turned and met emerald-green eyes set in a model-worthy face that stole my breath and jarred my memory hard—those same firm lips had slanted over mine. *No.* I wasn't going there.

But seriously… been there, done that before. I assessed him in record time. From the way he looked at me, I could tell he didn't recognize me—a very good thing, since our first encounter last summer hadn't been the best. For some reason, that look he gave me, as if he'd never seen me, pissed me off, regardless of the fact that he'd been drinking that night. It was not the same for me. He'd haunted my dreams and ruined the two kisses I'd had since.

The wall was *my hot guy* from the party. There was no way I would have forgotten that kiss. I remembered his name—Cole. There was no way I could forget that, either, even if I wanted to.

I took in every inch of his gorgeous face and his broad, muscular shoulders before I snapped out of it and frowned at the knowing smirk that curved his kissable lips.

A sound drew my focus to the three other guys standing

with him, including his brother, Damon, whom I knew from my short stint at a real job, and I frowned at how good-looking they all were. Full recognition filtered into my coffee-starved brain—seriously, there wasn't enough caffeine in the world for me to deal with this day.

I couldn't possibly forget the extent of their untouchable group, even if our interaction had been a mere few minutes and a year ago. Because these guys before me, and their leader, a.k.a. Brick Wall, they called themselves "the elite": Cole, Damon, and their cousins, Phoenix and Shane. They were exactly who I should have kept my distance from.

They were no different from the top tier at every shitty school I'd been to, with one exception—they were rich, power-ful, and beasts on the football field. I'd done my homework back then and again last night, even if hastily, and I was more than familiar with these assholes. They were monsters wrapped in beautiful packages, not to be confused with the regular teenage boys that every girl wanted and who guys wanted to be, and the sea of students I'd waded through were their minions.

"You must be the new girl," Brick Wall said. He shifted, crowding me, and I sensed stillness.

People were staring. *Yeah, I don't think so.* I took a slight step left, and his hand fell away from my elbow. I had a small space to squeeze through. A wicked grin curved his lips, and I bristled. He must have had inside information about who entered his domain, and I sure as hell wasn't giving him the satisfaction of a response. "Excuse me." I brushed past him, letting my backpack clip his side as I broke free from the circle of muscle.

Running into the school's top-tier jocks wasn't what I wanted or needed for my first day, no matter how much I wouldn't have minded repeating that kiss. Even my traitorous mind screamed *remember me.* He wouldn't because he'd been drunk that night, and I'd looked very different in my goth disguise.

It was for the best, because I didn't do the frat-boy-athlete type unless he was the son of a mark we were after. And I hoped he wasn't, because that was no boy back there, and my emotions were already in a tangled mess.

I hurried into a group of students entering the school, losing myself in the crowd, where I was most comfortable. I'd been taught to blend and be invisible, and that little altercation wasn't sitting right with me. Already, I'd caught the attention of the kids around us, and as I pushed farther into the hallway, the heat of Cole's gaze before the herd swallowed me, and I could disappear.

The school's entry echoed the wide doors and huge window that arched over it. The ceiling was vaulted with large wooden pillars. Lockers lined the walls, and I noted differences in the hallways as I went down them, searching for the registration office.

Once I found it, getting my schedule and locker assignment didn't take more than two minutes. After that, I located the nearest empty bathroom and pulled out the wallet I'd swiped from Brick Wall. *Let's see what he's got here.*

I turned away from the door and flipped open the wallet, pulling a wad of cash from inside but ignoring the black credit card. I couldn't help a grin from forming as I pocketed the money and scanned his ID. Cole Savage. His name was as hot and dangerous as he was. Good thing I planned to avoid the asshole jock. I memorized the address in case I needed it for whatever reason. It was always good to have information.

The door opened, and I closed the wallet, sensing someone behind me. Before I could move, a large hand fell on my shoulder, pinning me against the wall. Heat blanketed me, and tingles erupted along every exposed inch of skin. My backpack slid to the floor with a thump. I stiffened just before I was spun around, my back against the cold tile wall. *Fuck.* His hand whipped up and grabbed my face, fingers biting into my cheeks as he cupped my jaw. Everything in me stilled at the banked violence I sensed in him.

My heart beat a furious rhythm as Cole crowded me, anger darkening his green eyes to a crisp wintery evergreen. The heat from his solid, athletic body did things to me that I instinctively rebelled against as he pressed the length of his body into mine.

He released my face to fist his hand in the back of my hair, tilting my head so our gazes met as he plucked the wallet from my fingers and shoved it into his pocket, *minus the cash*. I smirked, wondering if he felt the weight difference before he put it away.

"Turnabout is fair play, little thief."

When his hand grasped my hip, I shifted to knee him in the balls, but he blocked me with a throaty laugh that did things to me I wasn't proud of. *Asshole.* Then his fingers dipped into my pocket. Goddammit. I squirmed to get free, but he held my schedule over my head. One shake while holding the corner of the folded sheet, and it opened.

"Riley Matthews." A sneer slanted across his mouth before he pressed the paper against my chest then bent so our faces were level. Fury clouded his gaze. "I prefer Little Thief. And you can keep the money," He dropped his gaze to roam from head to toe. "You obviously need it."

I whipped my head forward, intent on headbutting him, but he moved too quickly.

His banked anger flared, and his lips pulled back to issue a threat. "Be careful. I can make your life a living hell."

I held still at his parting threat. *What else is new?* When the bathroom door shut and I was alone again, I retrieved my backpack. I took a moment to calm down before my palms smacked against the door then realized I had to pull it, which only added to my simmering anger.

"Hot asshole, jock jerk."

A burst of laughter sounded to my left, and I whirled to face a girl slightly taller than my five-four. She had a wide smile, a cute pixie face, and edgy short brown hair to match her chic Parisian style.

"Yeah, Cole's all that and more." She winked. "I'm Cassie, and you must be new because I've never seen you here before."

"Riley." I relaxed and fell into step beside her on the way to what I hoped was the hall for psychology. Either way, I would follow her lead because it would be nice to have an ally for however long I attended this school. And it was my first day. Teachers would be lenient about being late this week.

"So you've met Cole. What about the rest of the crew?"

"Oh, there's a crew?" *That's what I'll be going up against.* I knew crews from some of the other schools I'd briefly attended. They were similar to gangs but without terrible violence. "Somehow, I pegged him for a spoiled rich kid, not a member of a posse." She laughed again, and a little more of my banked anger slid away.

"Nothing gang-like. That's not what I meant. But there are four of them, and since it seems you're on Cole's radar, you'll need to watch out for the pack of jacked-up she-wolves that circles the guys."

"Good to know. Thanks." Not that I'd let on, but I'd met them at the coffeehouse last summer. *Bring it on.* Something settled in me at the promise of a battle. I was always up for a challenge.

***

After school, I parked in the driveway next to the rental that would be home for however long. An ache radiated along my jaw from clenching my teeth too hard when I realized Mom's car wasn't there.

My head thumped against the headrest, and I let my mind

wander to the past. I missed her. Flipping through memories, I revisited one of our epic movie-marathon nights.

"Cards?" Mom scrunched her nose and tossed a handful of popcorn at me. "No, it's not my thing. I like running the personal-assistant scam. It's easier and less messy than the handful of relationship cons."

I fell back into the couch cushions, swiping her soda. I was too lazy to get another one, and she didn't care. We were both too wound up from the day's big score from her latest mark to pay attention to the romantic comedy playing on the small TV. Besides, we'd already seen *How to Lose a Guy in 10 Days* a bunch of times.

"Are we moving on soon? Or is it safe to keep going here?"

Mom had managed to write a few checks from petty cash and had buried the trail in the event planning she'd helped a large firm with under our latest alias. "Not yet." Her smile widened. "The news about the boss's latest mistress from his kid was gold. I think we can get some money from that angle too."

"Ew, are you going to sign up as mistress number two?" I couldn't imagine it. Mom was super careful about romance. We had rules about getting emotionally involved, and she adhered to them religiously.

She gagged, nabbed the soda, and took a long drink. "Gross. Don't even go there." She pulled one leg under her other and angled it so her back was against the armrest. "I meant faking a few messages from her."

"Ah." I loved that. "Let me guess… That's my job?" I couldn't wait. "I only have the basics. I'll pump Garrett for more details at school Monday. And I'm assuming you mean texts from the mistress?"

Mom pursed her lips. "Yeah. We need to figure out how to get the text to mimic her number."

"We've done that before. I'll text Uncle Ronan and get him

involved." I couldn't wait. The guy was a cheater. I could get on board big-time with screwing him over.

"Hey." She shoved at my shoulder. "How's school going? Do you like this one?"

I shrugged. "It's another school. Not much is different. You know how it goes. There are the usual hierarchies."

"Any cute boys? Or girls?" She slipped the questions in, not fooling me one bit.

"Nope. And even if there were, I wouldn't risk getting involved. I know the rules."

"What about the classes? And the online stuff? Is the laptop still working okay?"

"It works." It was old, but I didn't want to add pressure to get a newer one. "Nothing challenging with classes, either one. Why?" I had to do supplemental school under a completely different identity because she and Uncle Ronan worried I would slip through the cracks with learning, since we moved so much. I rarely finished a year or even a semester in the same school.

"I don't know." She looked pensive, and it instantly made me uncomfortable. "College is only a few years away. I need to figure something out."

"I don't have to go. You didn't."

Mom snorted. "Yeah, I got pregnant as a teenager and had to drop out of high school then go on the run with a baby. College was the last thing on my mind."

"Was it something you wanted to do?" I'd never considered it before. We ran cons all over the US but had so much fun together that I assumed she was content—aside from the fear of her ex, my dad, if he could be called that. I'd never met the guy and didn't plan to.

"No." her voice softened. "But I want you to be able to. And the dive team. Riles, you're so amazing. It's a gift. I want to figure out a way to eliminate the threat so you can have a real life."

Heat rushed to my face and settled in my cheeks. Mom and Uncle Ronan always said I was beautiful, but they had to say that—they loved me unconditionally. Mom was the beautiful one, not me. As for diving, I was good, but I wasn't sure if I was star-level great, like they always said. "I don't know about that, but as for college, I'll do an online one. Problem solved."

I didn't like her frown or the calculating gleam in her eyes. Mom never thought she was smart. The truth was, I got my brains from her. Classes, all of them, were easy. I never really struggled. Some were harder than others, but nothing academic caused me stress. And while she may not have graduated from high school or gone to college, she was the most brilliant person I'd ever met. She kept us out of *his* far-reaching grasp. And we'd never been busted for a single con. That said a lot.

"I want more for you, Riles. And I might have a way to make that happen. It'll just take some planning."

"I'm good, Mom. Really." I had everything I wanted. Out of all the kids I'd met at different schools, no one had a relation-ship with their parents like I did. I could tell her anything. She was always there for me. Why would I want that to change? By the way I could practically hear her mind working, I had a suspicion that if we did whatever she was concocting, things would change drastically.

I snapped back to the present. Things had changed already. It had to have been the plan she'd settled on, set into action. The problem was, I didn't like it. Not at all.

I let myself in and locked the door behind me. After yelling "Mom" and getting no response, I fell onto the couch and pulled out my phone.

Me: *Where are you?*

Three dots appeared by Mom's name, and a small sense of relief filled me. She wasn't dead.

Mom: *I'm in the city with Lucas. How was your first day at school? They have a pool!*

The fuck? Me: *Who the hell is Lucas?*

Mom: *Didn't Uncle Ronan tell you about him?*

Me: *He said you had a boyfriend, and that was who you were with. I call bullshit—what's going on?*

Mom: *I'll fill you in when I'm home. But... this is new. This year, do what you were meant to with diving. Things will be different here.*

She'd said that before we moved. I didn't believe it. I was too stunned to text for a moment.

How can I go against everything I've been taught?

No social media. No attention. Don't stand out. Blend into the background.

Now? She's permitting me to do what I always wanted.

Is it just a test? Can I trust my mother?

The temptation of having everything I'd ever wanted was just enough to make me think that maybe... maybe I could have it all.

CHAPTER FOUR

COLE

Voices echoed off the lockers, the sound competing with running water from the showers and the thud of equipment. I pulled my arm across my chest. I'd run extra drills and made my brother and cousins do the same after football practice. My body ached. It'd helped me but didn't do much for my brother. He needed something else. The locker room smelled of sweat and deodorant. I was ready to get out—not that the school's basement, where we met to spar, was any better.

I leaned against my locker as Brennan and Jackson headed to theirs, where Damon, Phoenix, and Shane were gathering our bags. We had about two seconds before our teammates were within hearing distance, and I could tell Damon needed to get more aggression out. My brother was always angry, which had worsened after Mom's death and the illusion that our dad was the root cause of her unhappiness exploded.

He wasn't the only one who could use some time in the ring. And I knew our cousins would follow, sensing the dam inside Damon threatening to burst, thanks to our father of the year and his selfish, cheating ways.

I fisted my hand in my brother's shirt and shoved him in the direction of the hallway as Jackson, the other starting tight end opposite me, threw his helmet into his locker and partially blocked our path.

"The new girl's hot," Jackson said to Brennan as he sat on the bench to pull off his cleats, his back to where we were.

Brennan smirked. "She'll be even hotter underneath me this weekend."

"You asked her out?" Jackson paused before pulling off his practice jersey, irritation tightening his voice.

A spike of possessiveness shot through me. I knew who the new girl was. I couldn't stop seeing her face

I hated that I wasn't remotely immune to her allure. Her skin had been so soft beneath my fingertips as I'd gripped her face. I could still smell lilac and honey, mixed with the faint twinge of chlorine, as I breathed her in. I didn't like her hold over me, not one bit. And it was apparent that she tempted the guys on the team. She was gorgeous. There was no way she'd remain under the radar for long.

I clenched a fist and fought the urge to slam it into Brennan's face. There was a familiarity about her that teased the edge of my mind, but I couldn't place why. It didn't matter. I might have been undeniably attracted to her, but she posed a problem. So no, Brennan wouldn't get an opportunity with her. And New Girl didn't know it yet, but she would be mine in whatever manner I wanted her to be, and I needed to send a clear message for the other guys to back the hell off.

Brennan stilled, his cleat dangling from his hand as I stood over him, my brother sliding out of focus. Not wanting them to see too much, I forced a laugh. "She's hot, but she's not worth the trouble." My brother and cousins crowded behind me, obviously sensing something off about my reaction. Brennan's gaze jerked from mine to theirs and back again.

"You asked her out?" Jackson repeated, his back to us as he tossed his stuff in the locker.

"Not yet. We have first period together. She sits in front of me." Brennan stood as he answered, half watching me but not close enough to realize how angry I was getting.

"She's got that long hair that I'm going to enjoy wrapping around my fist. And that ass. Fuck, that girl is fine."

Something snapped inside me, and I rushed Brennan, slamming him into the locker. "She's off-limits." With effort, I reeled it in and backed away a step so he could turn toward me, his eyes wide. "Spread the word."

He held up his hands, palms facing us. "I didn't mean to poach if you're interested in her, Cole. I thought you and Piper were a thing. I had no idea you liked the new girl."

Piper and I weren't anything, despite what she thought. Sure, we'd been sort of exclusive for half of last year, but that was over, and she knew it. I grunted then turned abruptly, heading for the hallway with the guys trailing behind. They were going to ask what the hell was up with my reaction. I couldn't explain. Little Thief was trouble, and I couldn't get her out of my mind.

We headed to the basement, where mats were set up in an unused corner that no one but us used. I'd sweet-talked the night staff into letting me borrow the key. I'd said it was to get something for our coach, but I'd made a copy. Ever since, we had a way in. It was where we practiced for the underground fights that happened a few times a year—usually not during football season, but something was up with my brother, and I could tell we would have to arrange one or two during the season.

We could've practiced at our home gym, since it was big enough, but Damon and I didn't want our dad to know about the fights on the off chance that he was paying attention.

Damon raised his brows. "What's going on with you and the new girl?"

"Nothing... yet." I didn't know why I wasn't sharing everything, but I wanted to keep our interaction close. "Just keep the guys away from her."

"Sure thing." He shrugged.

Shane grinned as he dropped his bag on the floor and took out his boxing gloves. "I'm going against you." He pointed at Damon.

It wasn't long until we sparred, working up another sweat. It felt good to burn off some of the excess energy. An hour later, we packed up and were heading to the lockers for a shower when I heard a splash from the pool down the hall. After showering, I went to investigate as the guys headed home.

Their voices grew fainter as I exited the locker room and headed for the pool. The sound of someone swimming echoed, and I slipped into the overly humid room, glad I hadn't put my shirt on yet, as a slight figure with dark hair climbed the high dive. A quick scan showed she was the only one here, which was odd. It was after hours, and the coaches and school administration would never let someone dive or even be in the pool without a staff member present.

I moved soundlessly to where the bleachers partially hid me. She finished the climb quickly before pausing at the end of the diving board. She was slender but curvy enough to make me do a double take. And I took in everything about her, from how her one-piece bathing suit highlighted her firm breasts to the water droplets trailing down her toned legs. Riley, my little thief.

She exhaled, and stillness settled around her. I found myself holding my breath. Then she launched herself off the board in a graceful arc, her body twisting and turning in ways that kicked my pulse into overdrive. She was a good thirty or so feet high, and I was mesmerized by the way she effortlessly moved. Her hands pierced the water, her body flowing behind them, barely making a ripple. Air whooshed from my mouth. My bag precariously dangled from my hand, almost forgotten. That dive... I'd witnessed something extraordinary from the girl with whom I had a score to settle.

It changed nothing. I would put a target on her back.

CHAPTER FIVE

RILEY

Awareness danced over my skin as I climbed out of the pool and eyeballed the half-naked asshole I'd run into that morning. I knew who he was. Water sloshed off my body in rivers to pool at my feet as I stood at the edge. My gaze collided with the school jock, one of four supposed gods in this place. Everyone in the school fawned over them.

But not me. I couldn't care less. Both interactions we'd had, even though he didn't remember the first, hadn't endeared him or his alpha personality to me. I fought to keep my eyes on his. Why did he have to invade my space without a shirt on? It took a Herculean effort on my part not to check out those wide shoulders, his python arms, and the washboard abs I wanted to run my tongue over. I'd never been happier to have water droplets running off me because they disguised the drool at the corner of my mouth.

With a dismissiveness that I didn't feel, I turned my back on him and returned to the diving board, pretending he wasn't there. It was impossible, but there was no way I would let him know his presence unsettled me.

A slight chill threaded through the humid pool room, which

I attributed to his presence and not the absence of bodies helping to heat the space. I was never more aware of the lack of clothes I wore than at that moment.

"How did you get in here?" His deep voice echoed throughout the space, seeming louder than it probably was.

I shot him a glare before delivering a flippant answer. "The door was unlocked."

Confusion pinched the corners of his mouth, and I smirked, enjoying every second of his reaction. Another rung up the ladder, and I was almost to the top.

Goose bumps rose on my arms and legs as I stepped off the ladder and onto the high dive. Mom hadn't been kidding about this being an excellent place for my senior year. And if I could show what I could do—for once—then I would get a scholarship at a Division-I school, which was my goal.

Not many schools had ten-meter boards, but this one did. Soon, I would look for a spot to cliff dive, too—I craved that feeling of flying through the air, my body twisting and turning before cutting through the water.

It was more freeing than anything else. When I dived, I controlled my fate. There were no worries, no fear about who could find us if I slipped up. As soon as my feet left the platform, I was in another world, In complete control. I wanted the sensation to last forever.

I needed it like my next breath.

Cliff diving would give me more of that. For the time being, I would stick close to home and practice at school, after hours and alone. I refused to look to see whether he'd left. I didn't need to, since his presence was a force impossible to miss.

At that last thought, my gaze flicked unbidden to the star tight end. I was pretty sure football practice had ended at least an hour ago. *Why is he here?*

I was too aware of him, but I refused to let my gaze crawl over every exposed inch of him. My gaze went rogue, and I sought him out. A spike of adrenaline infused my blood when our eyes collided. Dammit, I hated how he affected me. Why he was standing there, staring at me with no shirt on, was the question. He was a major distraction.

I took a deep breath, released it slowly, and did what I always did during a meet or a serious dive during which I was trying something new. Air slowly pushed from my mouth as I found my center, picturing every twist and turn my body would execute when I stepped off the board. When that sense of calm surrounded me, I pushed off, floating for half a second before executing somersaults and twists.

A loud sound pierced my concentration. My body jerked the tiniest bit, and I hit the water hard. My calves stung from over-rotating and slamming into the water at an odd angle. Pushing through the pain, I arched, reaching for the surface, then kicked hard until I broke through. A few strokes and I was at the ladder, hauling myself out. A red haze coated my vision as I stalked the asshole.

I crowded him, slapping my hand hard against his chest. He didn't move an inch. I pushed harder. He only stared, and my rage detonated.

"Your stupid stunt could have seriously hurt me." An angry vibration traveled through me, and my fingers splayed over his hard pecs, my nails biting into his skin, I hoped hard enough to draw blood.

He leaned down, eliminating the height distance between us to the point that I could count the gold flecks in his eyes. He dwarfed me in size and muscle at about six foot two inches. I took in his almost-black hair and chiseled face, which I could see gracing the pages of men's fashion magazines. And I wasn't even going to acknowledge how a few drops of water lazily rolled over his eight-pack abs from where my hands were still pressed.

"Then you shouldn't be in here doing something so dangerous." His gaze flicked down, visually caressing every inch of my body. "Alone."

I couldn't process that. Not now. We were too close. I felt the heat from his body radiating into mine, affecting me in traitorous ways. Snatching my hands back as if burned, I bared my teeth then growled. "Get the hell out of my way."

He didn't move an inch. I shifted to the side, grabbed the towel and backpack I'd left, then stomped past him, avoiding the bag near his feet. My shoulder clipped his but didn't do a damn thing to him.

A bruise would form on my calves, and I had every intention of snapping a picture of it as evidence, a little something to use against him if I needed it.

I slammed my hands against the metal bar on the door. It swung open, and I stormed out to the sound of his mocking laughter.

Asshole. I hated the guy, and now, I wasn't going to be able to get the sight of him without a shirt on out of my head.

CHAPTER SIX

COLE

Only one other car was in the garage—my brother's, not our dad's. I was used to his absenteeism, but it still made me angry. Since Damon's was the only other vehicle parked here, Phoenix and Shane must have gone home after football practice and sparring rather than to our house for dinner.

I let myself into the house to find Damon at the kitchen island, scarfing down some reheated lasagna from the night before. My stomach growled. Louisa's food was Michelin-star quality, and we did whatever she asked to get her to make our favorites. The lasagna was one of them.

"You better not have finished it all." I was in a shit mood, unable to get the image of Riley out of my mind. Her bathing suit left little to the imagination. And while I could tell she had a rockin' body from our run-in on the first day of school, every inch of her was burned into my thoughts after what happened earlier.

Damon smirked. "I saved you a piece."

"It had better be a big one." I yanked open the fridge, rattling the contents on the door, then riffled through a few containers until I found a good-sized portion in Tupperware. "You're lucky."

"What's your problem? Something happened from school to here to cause your attitude to go to hell?"

Yeah, but I wasn't in the mood to share. "No, just hungry. Where is everyone?" I cracked the lid before putting the food in the microwave, setting the time, and pressing Start.

Damon shrugged. "Louisa went home, and I haven't seen Dad since last week. He went on a business trip, right?"

"Something like that." Business combined with personal, no doubt.

"When will he be home?" Damon asked. "Not that it matters."

"Not sure." My phone pinged at the same time as the microwave. I had priorities, though, and got my food onto a plate and dug in before checking to see who the message was from. Not even a minute later, my phone rang. I pulled my phone from my pocket and checked to see who it was. Dad. My fork clattered onto the plate as I leaned back in the chair and put in my Bluetooth earbuds.

"Cole."

"Dad." I could already tell from his voice that he would be a pain in my ass. Damon grimaced.

"Did you get the alarm notification on the rental property?"

"Yeah." I clicked through the alerts and located it again to look closely at who the girl was. I hadn't cared before. "I was going to check on it after I got something to eat." I should have done it before school when I'd gotten the alert, but whoever it was had gone, so…

"No need to go there. It's just my girlfriend's daughter."

I rolled my eyes at that one. *Wow, he's openly admitting his sugar-daddy status now? Way to go.* "Got it." His comment didn't need an answer. But that never mattered. If I hadn't acknowledged him, he would have dug into me for a half hour to satisfy whatever power trip he was on. After the long day I'd had, I didn't need his particular brand of torture.

Damon scarfed down the last of his food then hurried to rinse the plate and stick it in the dishwasher before rushing from the room. I glared at his retreating back. *Coward.*

"How's football?"

"Good. Coach thinks the game will be a sweep."

"And your brother? Is he staying out of trouble?"

"He already ate dinner and went to start on homework. We're good." *What's his deal?*

"Why aren't you doing your homework? Both of you need to make sure your grades are top-notch. I saw that A-minus you got on the calculus test. That won't cut it, Cole."

Unusual for him to check, but it probably hadn't even been him. He had his secretary doing all sorts of shady shit. Weekly reports on his kids to make it look like he paid attention to us was a part of that. And on that note, I needed information on his plans, specifically when to expect him to grace us with his presence. "When are you coming home?"

"In a day or two. Just wrapping up some business."

Sure you are... We talked for another minute before I was free to hang up and take a closer look at the alert. I wanted to know who the girl was and if I knew her. With a few clicks, I had the app pulled up with the correct video feed. The video started with the door opening and a slight figure with long, dark hair emerging from the house. Her head was down, and it was hard to get a clear view of her face, but something tugged at my memory. The way she slung her backpack over one shoulder and the gentle sway of her hips... *Holy shit, I know who that is— my little thief.*

As soon as I placed who she was, a wave of anger had me gritting my teeth. What the hell was she doing mixed up with my dad? Dark laughter filled the room before I realized it was my own. Dad wasn't due home for a day or two. It was the perfect time to pay her a little visit.

I left my food uneaten on the island to retrieve the key. It would be there for me to finish when I got back—or not. Damon would consider it fair game if he came across it before I got home. I didn't care about that or the emptiness in my gut.

With single-minded focus, I got back in my car and headed to the office that managed Dad's rental properties. I knew Cindi would be in, since she worked the evening shift. Dad had hired a twenty-four-hour service. When I pulled up to the stand-alone one-story building, I forced myself to relax before knocking on the glass door. It took a minute until the door buzzed with the release of the security lock. I wasted no time in yanking it open and navigating the desks until I was at Cindi's. She was close to Dad's age, loved bright lipstick, and had huge brown eyes and matching hair with gray streaked through it that she proudly wore.

"Hey, Hon. What brings you in?" A wide smile stretched her pumpkin-orange lips.

"The new renters are locked out, and since Dad is friends with them, he asked me to pick up the spare key."

"Sure thing, but I'll have to have them fill out a form. Just for record keeping."

"Of course. I'll bring that with and drop it off later." I made a point of leaning toward the steaming cup of hazelnut coffee on her desk. "That smells incredible. You always make the best coffee."

"Well, aren't you sweet." Her smile widened, showcasing two dimples on her softly aging face. "I have some to-go cups in the back if you would like to take one with you."

I grinned. "You're the best."

She chuckled then eased out of her chair and slowly made her way to the back room. A twinge of guilt struck as I noted the stiffness of her gait. I could have gotten it myself, but that would have defeated the purpose of stopping by. When she was out of sight, I went around her desk and hurriedly typed in the property address where Dad's girlfriend and her kid were staying. As soon as it came up, I scanned the information. My teeth snapped together, and I clenched my jaw hard at what I found.

Raelyn and Riley Matthews were living there rent free. That told me everything I needed to know about the little freeloaders. It made Riley more of a target than when she'd stolen my wallet.

I heard Cindi finishing up with the lid, backtracked out of the program, then returned to where I been on the other side of the desk.

"Here you go. We're out of those cardboard sleeves, so be careful. It's hot." Then she unlocked her drawer, found a copy of the key, and handed me the form I would have to forge. "Bring that back as soon as you can, Cole."

"You're an angel." I toasted her with the coffee before turning toward the door. Once in my car, I eased out of the parking lot so I wouldn't send a red flag to Cindi then pointed the Range Rover in the direction of the ranch on the edge of Hidden Valley.

Wind rushed through the open windows as I sped down the streets. Fifteen minutes later, I parked along the curb in front of the modern rental property. The blinds shielded my ability to see inside, and when I curved my fingers around the doorknob, I found it locked. But I had a way in. I took the spare keys from my pocket. After unlocking the door, I crept through the entryway, past the open-plan kitchen and living room, and followed the heavy thump of music from down the hallway where the bedrooms were.

No one else was home, since her mom was in the city with my dad. That meant I had as much time as I needed to fuck with her in a space that she thought was safe. Without making any noise, I found the source of the music in the back bedroom and leaned against the doorjamb.

Little Thief was lying on her stomach on a fluffy white duvet that covered the bed, head down as she read a book. Her long, dark-brown hair curtained her face. A sensual beat of the drums from some indie song crooned from a Bluetooth speaker on the dresser, and she rocked her legs back and forth. From my position, I had a glimpse down her shirt. Firm breasts strained against the loose cotton. Everything about her was toned and sexy as hell.

The tip of a pen rested against her full bottom lip, and she occasionally tapped it against the pillowy softness. I had to reach down and adjust myself at the thought of what her mouth would feel like wrapped around my dick. She was hot, and I badly wanted a taste. Too bad she would be gone soon enough, once my dad was through with her mom. Given his track record, that would be a couple of months, tops.

She was in the perfect position for me to grab the back of her hair, flip her onto her back, and peel her clothes off. The front of my pants tightened uncomfortably. I must have made a noise because Little Thief's head whipped up, and wide brown eyes met mine.

"What the hell are you doing here, stalker?" She launched herself off the bed, clutching her pen in her fist like a weapon.

"You going Jason Bourne on me?" I dropped my gaze to the pen in her clenched hand.

"If needed." She bared her teeth, growling through them. "I repeat: what the hell are you doing here?"

I opened my hand, letting the keys dangle from the ring wrapped around my middle finger. "I have a key."

"Why?" She jerked back a step. "Did the rental get mixed up, double-booked? Because if it did, you'll have to find somewhere else to live. Now."

"I would ask if this was what you spent my money on, but I

found out more about you. And your mother. Seems you didn't need to steal from me for a place to live." *Your whore of a mother worked that out for you.* I would keep that part to myself for the time being.

The sneer she had on her face as she looked me up and down was downright lethal, and I was impressed. "I didn't need your money." She smirked and crossed her arms over her chest, still gripping that fucking pen. "I took it because I could."

So she thinks I'm an easy target? Well, Little Thief, you're in for a hell of a ride. "Good to know." I let my gaze rove lazily over her body, lingering on my favorite parts. "We'll get up close and personal over the next few weeks."

"Yeah, I don't think so." Her eyes shot daggers at me.

I couldn't remember the last time I'd had so much fun. I still didn't like her on principle. After all, she had stolen from me, and her mom was dating my dad. If my dad didn't dump her mom soon, I would ensure she and her kid weren't around for long. But before their breakup and her fleeing town, I could have some fun. "Want to know why we'll be in each other's space for more than just school?"

"Hardly." She flicked her hair over her shoulder, raising her chin.

Cute. "Your mom is dating my dad." I flashed her a wolfish grin, promising all that would follow. "I guess we're going to be stepbrother and sister, since our parents are together, and I'll have access to that tight little body"—I shook my hand, letting the keys jingle—"whenever I want."

All the color leached from her face, and a visible tremble rocked her. I pivoted on my heel and left the same way I'd come, the look on her face worth the not-right feeling the taunt gave me.

CHAPTER SEVEN

RILEY

As soon as that fucker left, I shoved a chair under the doorknob of the front door then paced the length of the foyer, my phone pressed against my ear, willing Mom to pick up. *Come on.* Another glance at the driveway confirmed that the devil was gone for now.

He has a key.

I couldn't process the shit Mom had gotten me into with this con. And that was what it had to be because there was no way I would believe her relationship with *Cole's father* was anything other than fake.

"Hello?" Mom answered. "Riles?"

I sagged against the wall, wanting to tell her everything but also just missing her. So instead of complaining, I pushed all the angst aside—temporarily. "Hi, Mom." I leaned my head back against the wall. "What's going on? You haven't been here since the night we moved in."

She'd done that before, but I'd been in on everything. The con. The players. Every detail of what she'd thought up. I'd known her part and mine, backward and forward. It was our thing. We'd plan, review every possible scenario, and create multiple exit strategies based on potential problems. I couldn't help from feeling shut out and betrayed.

The other thing that didn't sit right with me was that the only other time she'd kept me in the dark was in California, in this town, a year ago.

"I know." She sighed then must have covered the phone because her words were muffled. A door shut before she spoke. "Didn't Uncle Ronan tell you everything?"

I snorted because that was a cop-out if I'd ever heard one. "Yeah, but it was a little hard to believe. A boyfriend? A legitimate one? We don't do that—*you* don't do that."

"I know this is hard to believe, but try, okay? For me?" Silence stretched between us, and I refused to fill it. "I didn't expect anything to happen when I met Lucas, but there was a connection. And for once in my life, I wanted to give myself the opportunity to see if I could have something real and healthy with a man. Can you understand that?"

No, not even a little. Well, maybe a little, but I wasn't ready to give in.

"How's the new school?"

I snorted again. Were we doing that? Pretending everything was okay? I sank my teeth into my lower lip before releasing it with a sigh. Maybe the boyfriend was listening. "It's school. Same as always but fancier."

Her infectious laughter trilled through the speaker, and I wished even more that she wasn't far away. "Did you check out the pool? The diving board is ten meters. That's the highest of any school you've been to."

"I know. You told me already. And yeah, I checked it out."

"So you're going out for the team?"

I rolled my eyes. There was no point. "Why? We'll be moving before the season's over."

"Not this time. Go out for the team, Riley. Things are different. I promise. When you meet Lucas—"

"Mom." I couldn't do it anymore. I was agitated. "You're dating Cole's dad?" A renewed flash of anger swept through me, especially because of the bullshit I'd just endured from him breaking into the house.

"Yeah. You met him?" The lightness that had laced her voice drained away.

"What's the matter?"

Good. This isn't even a little bit funny. "Unfortunately."

"It can't be that bad, Riles. Give it some time. I'm sure everything will work out."

Who is this woman? A pang sliced through me. She was my best friend, and I wanted her there, commiserating and scheming with me. A ping sounded, and I pulled the phone away from my ear, switching it to speaker so I could check my texts.

I didn't recognize the number, but the text was an invite to the pep rally to celebrate the football team tonight, and it was a bonfire.

"That sounds like fun. You should go."

I must have read it aloud. "Ugh, hard pass."

"Riley, go. Have some fun. Cole and his brother are on the team. They're star players."

"I do not care about them in any capacity." I scowled at her enthusiastic response. "Why? What's the angle here?"

"There is none. Be a normal teenage girl for a change. Go to a school event, a party. Whatever."

"But I'm not normal. I have never been, and you know why." None of this was normal—we were always on the same page. I couldn't get my head around what was different about this town, this guy, that was making her into someone I didn't know. "Let's leave this town. I can get a job. The con can be done now." I had to try.

"We're not leaving." Something squeaked, and I could imagine her dropping into a chair, wherever she was, and pulling her knees to her chest just like I was. We'd done that so many times before that I could see it as clearly as if she were across from me.

Another text came through, and I shoved the image of my mom from my head for a moment so I could focus on what had come through. When I saw the picture on my screen, I pushed off the floor and paced in the small foyer. Shit. The image was of me getting out of the school's pool when I wasn't supposed to be there. The clock on the wall behind me showed clearly as day that it was after hours. I knew who the text was from—Cole.

I fired off a text: *Go fuck yourself.*

His response was immediate, and my skin prickled in response. *Not if I fuck you first.*

Ugh. *Get over yourself, stalker.*

All I could do was think about sex with him and his very hard, developed body. I couldn't get the images of what it would be like to feel his body surrounding mine from my head. And I didn't feel as disgusted as I should.

That was it. I had to convince my mom to give up whatever game she had going on—the one she hadn't included me in. "I know you better than anyone else. Even better than Uncle Ronan." He didn't even know half the stuff we did to survive. "What's really going on?" I slid back to the floor. "You dumped me in this town, and haven't been here since the night we moved in. This isn't normal, not even for us."

That heavy silence settled over the connection again, but I wouldn't break it. She had to be the one.

"I have my reasons." She sounded like her old self for the first time since she'd answered the phone. "We'll talk about them when I'm home."

Finally, I knew there was something more to what she was doing.

CHAPTER EIGHT

COLE

"Be reasonable, Joe," Aunt Cece pleaded as she sat at the kitchen table in the scrubs she'd worn to work a double shift at the hospital.

Phoenix had been first into their house, but Shane, Damon, and I were on his heels. Their mom was usually asleep at that time of day, so we'd entered quietly.

She had her phone on speaker, resting on the kitchen table. Her back was to us, so she didn't notice us. We paused when Phoenix stopped. He pulled his phone out of his pocket and hit the button to record. I would have done it too. I reached for my phone to do the same, but he already had his in hand.

"How the hell did you get this number?"

"Your assistant connected me when I told her you were late with—as in I never received—child-support payments. She was very reasonable when I told her I bet the NFL would be interested to know about it." We stayed silent as her voice grew louder.

"Listen very closely, Cecilia." A warning coated his harsh words, and our cousins stiffened even more. I knew they were bracing for impact because I was too. That asshole wouldn't get away with this. "I gave you the house when you told me you were pregnant. If you need money, sell that."

"I will not sell the boys' home out from under them. They love it here, and it's close to their cousins. I haven't asked you for a goddammed dime ever."

"But you are now."

"Yes."

I could picture her saying that through gritted teeth. Aunt Cece was practical and sweet, a giver—she was an ER nurse. But there was a limit where her kind heart couldn't take anymore, and then anger took over. I'd seen it more than once. It was what gave her the strength to be the incredible mom she was to our cousins, something her sister—my mom—had lacked. I could never figure out why that was. My mom was weak and selfish. Theirs had gotten all the good qualities.

"I will repeat this and clarify it for you, so pay close attention. I gave you the house, and that's enough. I'll slap a restraining order against you if you contact me again. I don't even know if the brats are my kids, and you're lucky you got what you did."

"Don't be ridiculous. You know they're your twins. They look just like you. All I'm asking is that you help with their tuition when they go to college in two years. I'm not even asking for a dime of all the child support you should have paid over the years."

"We aren't married and never were. You don't have any ground to stand on. Do not call me again."

There was a click and half a second of silence before she let out a stream of curse words that would have made a sailor blush. I vibrated with fury, which was probably mild compared to how my cousins felt.

When she stormed out of the kitchen, still not noticing we were behind her, Phoenix whirled. He pointed at Shane, who went back to the door and slammed it as if we'd just gotten there.

Spilling into the kitchen, Shane yanked the pot roast from the fridge and tossed the entire thing, still in the container, in the microwave. With a few taps on the panel, it whirled to life, heating our lunch and the reason we'd come to their house in the first place. Aunt Cece had made the roast yesterday and told Phoenix and Shane to have us come over today and eat with them while she slept. Except she wasn't sleeping.

Nobody said a word while we got plates and drinks out. When it became apparent that she was in her room and wouldn't come out, Phoenix motioned for us to grab everything to take outside. We would eat by the pool, where we could talk freely without risking her overhearing.

Once outside, we set everything down, but no one ate.

"Maybe we should go to community college, so Mom doesn't feel so much pressure." Shane thrust his hands through his hair. "I could quit football and get a job too."

"Bullshit!" Phoenix said, exploding. "That fucker is going to pay when we're in the NFL. Neither of us is quitting. We'll come up with the money or go to Grandad if we have to."

"No." I would go to the ends of the earth for my cousins and brother. There was nothing I wouldn't do for them. "We'll increase the number of fights. And in college too. Damon and I don't need much of our winnings, and we have an account he and I put most of it into for you guys."

"What are you talking about?" Phoenix froze, his silvery eyes locked onto mine.

I shrugged because I didn't want to make a big deal about the money. The rest was a big fucking deal. "The NFL scopes Thane for the draft. It's the best place for all of us to be. You're both going. There is no community college option for you guys." I narrowed my gaze on Shane to make sure he got the message. "You want to get your dad back?"

"Fuck yeah," Shane growled. Phoenix nodded, his mercurial eyes showing his hatred.

"The scouts are out, and we're going to take our team to state, where we'll make damn sure to win. You three will do the same next year. Phoenix, I know they're looking at you already. But we're all playing for the team. There will be some sort of scholarship. Damon and I will help to cover the rest of the yearly fees. We've got your back." *Always.*

"And if we need to," Damon said, "we'll blackmail our dad into making him cover the balance. God knows he owes us."

"The fights are the best way for us to pull in bank. There won't be time to get a job, not with the team requiring forty hours a week on top of classes, homework, and studying."

They knew I was right, and slowly, their expressions eased. It was the best plan of action. Everything would be all right. I would make sure of it.

"So," Damon said, about to stir the pot. It was what he did best. "What are the plans for payback for Joe?"

An evil grin spread across Phoenix's face. "To be among the first round of draft picks. We'll spill everything when we're starters on a team, and he'll try to claim us as his kids because it'll help his career. And we have proof." He waved his phone. "I have a few of these conversations. We save them on a backup drive too."

Shane's malicious smirk matched his brother's, and I couldn't help but laugh. It was perfect.

"Our mom will look like the saint she is, and he'll look like the dirtbag who abandoned his pregnant girlfriend and his kids and denied support of any kind."

Good. With that settled, we dug into the food. My family was my world. I would do anything in my power to make sure they were safe and protected. They were the only things I cared about other than football.

I let my mind wander to the bonfire later that night,

glancing at the string of texts that had resulted from the threat I'd sent Riley. The event just got a hell of a lot more interesting.

Flashes of orange light flickered through the trees as I followed the path to where the pep rally for the football team was underway. It was not far from where we lived, so we chose to walk through the thick grouping of trees on the edge of our property then the mile to where Piper's house and the bonfire were.

Damon prowled beside me, already scanning the crowd through the trees as we headed toward the beach. Dark energy poured off him, matching mine. Our father had checked in again, speaking with Damon the second time. Whatever he said had lit a match under my volatile brother, and he'd slammed out of the house with me close on his heels.

Damon would need to let off steam for whatever fucked-up thing Dad had said, but I had other plans... mainly a girl with a hot body and a wicked mouth who needed to be put in her place. Her presence at the rental property spelled trouble for us, and I wasn't going to let that happen.

Dad had tried to move a woman in shortly after Mom died, and we'd made things so uncomfortable for her two brats that they'd fled to parts unknown. It was a message to him—we ruled the town, and no one would take Mom's place. She wouldn't have won any awards as a mother, but we loved her, and she would still be with us if he hadn't left for his piece of ass that weekend. And I was out of there in a year, but I wasn't leaving Damon to whatever fucking new family Dad thought he would replace us with.

That made Riley a target because I knew how Dad operated, and him being gone this long with his latest piece spelled trouble. The more damage I could do now to set the stage, the better. Little Thief would show if she didn't want me to release that picture to the diving coach.

When we broke through the tree line and crossed to the sand behind the few houses that separated us from the growing crowd, I scanned the sea of faces, looking for her. *She'd better make an appearance.* After a second pass, her absence was clear. I shifted toward the stage and the familiar group gathered there.

Farther down, waves crashed against the shoreline, just out of reach of the warm glow of the fire. The sky was inky and devoid of stars. Either from the glare of the orange flames or a heavy cloud cover.

"They're over there."

Damon refocused my attention, and I looked where he'd indicated, my steps in line with his as we made our way through the crowd of people who easily parted for us and toward our cousins.

Most faced the crackling flames and the shrill voices of the cheer squad as they hyped everyone up. I took in the way their uniforms clung to them, the skirts riding low to showcase their hip bones. Piper, Brook, and Tracey stood at the edge of the stage with Jessica and Teagan flanking them. Varying shades of blond hair, winged eyeliner, and bright-red lips rounded out their arsenal. The rest of the squad backed them up, but the main captains, Piper and Brook, ruled our school, just underneath us. And we let them, since they had their purpose for us.

Our group of guys hooked up a designated go-to girl from the squad when we wanted someone for a night or even an hour. They were always willing, which annoyed me more often than not. I let my gaze travel over Piper, with her long legs and generous breasts straining against her too-tight top, but nothing sparked. Not a hint of desire. It was why I'd broken things off with her at the end of last year, and she'd been trying to get me back ever since. But I didn't want to end up like Dad, and with her, I couldn't see a monogamous relationship lasting.

The crowd roared as Piper amped them up about our upcoming game against our rivals, Hidden Valley High, tomorrow night. Teagan spotted us before we ducked behind a group from our team. Phoenix and Shane were off to the side of the rest of the varsity players, and judging by the scowl on Phoenix's face, his mood matched mine. The full power of his glare was fixed on Tracey, who was doing a stellar job of sending Shane sultry glances. Shane may have preferred to stay oblivious about how much his brother hated his girlfriend, but the rest of us weren't.

We closed in on our cousins, standing next to them and slightly offset from the rest of the team. Damon pounded his fist against Shane's, and Shane grinned. Both fed off the crowd, but Damon's darkness crackled around the edges, and I caught Phoenix's eye with a warning. If we didn't watch my brother closely, blood would spill, and that was better saved for the upcoming fight. I just needed to keep him restrained for the next couple of days.

When his searching gaze settled on Jessica, I relaxed. She would keep him busy. Another few minutes passed as the girls squealed in their pep talk that I didn't bother to listen to. Things seemed like they would be okay with Damon, at least until Derek whistled then made a crude comment to Jessica and a few of the girls. I couldn't have cared less—usually, Damon wouldn't, either, but tonight was different. I noted his intent before he even moved.

I took a step to the right and pivoted until I faced him. Leaning forward, I held his gaze. "Rein it in for one more day. Take it out on the field against HVH."

"Fuck you," Damon growled.

Shane and Phoenix closed ranks to minimize the view as I fisted his shirt and pulled him close. He didn't give a shit about the girl, but any excuse to fight was a good one for him. I knew my brother well.

"This isn't the time." I kept him tethered until the hot anger was reduced to a simmer. "Get laid then focus on the game against those fuckers from HVH." The cheer squad revved up the crowd more then introduced the football team to a volley of "woot, woot, woot" from the pumped-up mass of people clutching Solo cups on the beach.

"Fine," Damon groused. "Let's get this bullshit over with."

I slapped his shoulder, holding him back so I could let him know my plans for tonight. "Riley should be here."

"Diver girl?" Shane laughed.

I'd shared that I'd found her at the pool diving the other night. Damon knew the score with the rental, and all our cousins needed was a reminder that she was mine to fuck with and they needed to freeze her out. I didn't want anyone dating her. "You find her before I do. Deliver her to me."

I released Damon then took the stage with Phoenix. My brother and Shane flanked Phoenix and me as we took our place at the mic in front of the cheer squad. I let the energy from the crowd feed into me, and I knew the guys around me were doing the same. The rest of our team gathered close to the stage then faced out toward the swarm of students there either to support us or party. That was what my brother and cousins were impatient to get started, and I couldn't blame them—time to put this pep bullshit to bed.

"Tomorrow night, we go against our rivals," I shouted into the mic, letting the crowd feel my determination and barely leashed violence. "They want the victory, but we'll never let them take it from us."

A roar went through the crowd, and I grinned at the sheer velocity. I continued to look for her from my vantage point above everyone else. Then I spotted her on the crowd's edge, looking like she would run. Not happening. It was time to put a quick end to this bullshit. "Tonight, we party. Tomorrow, we take what's rightfully ours—victory—and send those fuckers back where they belong!"

Solo cups shot into the air with hoots and hollers. The four of us jumped off the makeshift stage, and beer was passed along the players until it reached our hands. Damon grabbed Jessica from the stage, lifted her down, then headed toward the dark section of the beach behind us. I watched him for a few minutes before he disappeared from sight.

With him occupied, I focused on why I wanted to come in the first place and maneuvered away from my cousins. Phoenix had his arm around some pep girl, and as usual, Shane was locked at the hip with Tracey. I stepped around Shane, intent on getting to Riley, when a small hand latched on my arm, then a soft body pressed against my side. The overpowering floral perfume that cut through the smokiness from the bonfire told me who it was without even needing to look. "No."

"What? Come on, Cole. I put all this together for you." She attempted to hide the bite of anger from my rejection with her bubbly laugh, but the half moons forming on my bicep told otherwise.

"I'm not interested, Piper." Then I leveled her with a cold stare. "Back off." She was turning into a stage-five clinger, something we all avoided. I hadn't hooked up with her since the end of last year, and still, she hadn't let up. Soon, I would need to stop her possessiveness, but I wasn't looking forward to the fallout from whomever decided to take her place. There was always someone, and I guessed that it would be Teagan. She'd been eyeing me like her next meal ticket for the past six months, especially since Phoenix had stopped showing any interest and shut her down cold. Scouts had been showing up consistently to our games, and that made some of the girls rabid.

"You don't mean that." Piper pushed a greater portion of her breast against me as she placed her other hand on my chest then trailed the tips of her fingers lower. "I'll make it good for you."

She pushed up onto her toes and leaned into me even more. "You know I'm the best."

I didn't bother answering. I just shook her off and shoved her into Craig, our defensive back. By the time I'd gotten free of Piper's octopus arms, I'd lost track of Riley. She wasn't standing on the edge anymore. Shit. My mood shifted from bad to worse. *She better not have left. Not yet, anyway.*

Piper's irritating voice faded the farther I went, but her situation remained in the back of my mind. Rumors were floating around, mainly among the cheerleaders, that things were shaky between Piper's parents. All I knew was that her dad, who was in business with Tracey's, had contacted mine not long ago, which might have caused her to up her game. She knew where I was headed and what my goals were. Everyone did. Piper was smart. She didn't need me to have the future she wanted. She could make that happen all on her own.

I planned to get my degree in business—not law, as my dad assumed—at Thane University, and after graduation, the NFL. Piper was the cheer squad captain, and I had no doubt that she wanted to ride my train and become an NFL wife. It wasn't happening. I couldn't stand her on a good day, but she had been a decent lay until she thought we were dating. Freshman year, I slept around and kept things casual. Then we hooked up, but I didn't date—never had and didn't plan to. I'd seen too much destruction between our parents to want anything like that.

She would have blended into the night if she'd been just another foot or two away from the reach of the bonfire's glow, but I caught a glimpse of long, wavy hair that came almost to her tiny waist. Faded jeans hugged her tight ass and adhered to her curves in a way that made me jealous. Her form-fitting gray T-shirt ended an inch above the waistline of her jeans, showing a sexy slash of toned skin.

My body heated at the sight of her. It was the end of August.

The days were still warm, but the temperature dropped at night, making jeans the better choice over shorts.

When I broke through a group of girls that stood between us, I jerked to a stop. Riley wasn't alone, as I'd expected her to be. Instead, she was talking to some guy. I wasn't sure who he was—maybe the swim team's captain. He had the build of a swimmer with his broad shoulders, trim waist, and long arms. All I knew was that he didn't hang with the football team.

She laughed at something he said. Her head went back, and her sensual, throaty laugh filled the air, making my cock jump in a way I hadn't expected. *What is it with this chick?*

A rush of possessiveness filled me, and I strolled up to the two of them and threw my arm around her shoulders. The look I gave the guy told him everything he needed to know about who she belonged to—and it wasn't him. The tool standing before us made some stuttering excuse and took off.

She whirled in my arms, and I pulled her tighter to me, feeling her body against mine. It was enough to distract me from the message I wanted to deliver. She was small and tight but soft in all the right places. Lips so soft I could feast on them for days. I wanted her like my next breath, a thought that should've disturbed me more than it did.

She tried to shove me off her. I wasn't moving even an inch, and she was too tiny to make me. The beer fell from my hand so I could use both of them on her.

"What the hell was that?" she growled, shoving harder. "Get the fuck off me."

I bent my head enough so I could whisper in her ear. A mixture of hate and heat vibrated between us, hotter than anything I'd ever felt. "Go ahead and struggle a bit more. I like it." I pulled her closer so she could feel how hard I was for her. "It only turns me on."

The way she smelled, so sweet and tempting, toyed with my mind. Every inch of me vibrated for her.

I had to have her. There was nothing between us but fucked-up desire and soul-deep hatred, but she was firmly etched into my thoughts, and there was only one way to get her out. I was salivating at how much I wanted to sink into her tight heat, feel her writhe beneath me, and hear her moan my name as she begged me to make her come. That day would come sooner than she thought.

Her head canted back so that our heated gazes locked and held. Disgust tugged her full lips into a sneer, and I flashed her a matching one before I delivered the message I'd planned on since demanding her presence tonight.

"As you can see, this is my court. I control everything that happens in the school and outside of it. No matter how far you try to run, you'll end up right back here, trapped." I fisted my hand in her long, thick hair, giving the strands a gentle tug, just enough for her to know I was in control of everything tonight, even her. "There's nowhere you can go. Might as well face it, Little Thief. You're already mine."

RILEY

This was a mistake. I struggled against Cole but wasn't able to move an inch. He'd grabbed my hair, and an arm locked around my waist like a steel band. I should have taken the chance that he'd been bluffing with that picture and not come here.

Every inch of me was pressed against his hard body. We were a good distance away from the crackling bonfire, but heat radiated from him. My breath came in quick puffs. *Why does this asshole have such a hot body?* I fought to remain rigid when I wanted to melt against him. There was no denying it—I wanted him.

But there was no way I could give in to his twisted demands.

He leaned down and brushed his lips against my ear. I shivered, almost combusting into a puddle at his feet, helpless against how he made me feel. So damn hot.

When he straightened, I caught the wicked gleam reflecting in his eyes. "I like it when you squirm against me."

Oh, hell no. I gave myself a mental slap because that train of thought was wrong—in so many ways. I sank my nails into his chest and pushed against him, leaning my head back as far as I could, given the restriction of his hand in my hair. "I'll never be yours, asshole."

The gentle sound of the waves breaking against the shore vied with the blood rushing through my veins. More of our surroundings faded as his erection dug into my stomach, but I wasn't afraid. He was all bluster. *I hope.*

Things could change. Maybe. I didn't think it would come to that. To be sure, I let him know who he was messing with. "If you try to stick that thing in any part of me, I'll rip your balls off and shove them down your throat."

The deep rumble of his laughter climbed up his chest, vibrating into me before bursting from his mouth. "You'll be too busy begging me for more." He tugged on my hair then whispered in my ear. No words came. His nose trailed a sensitive path along my throat, awakening every nerve ending until they were hyperaware before he whispered, "And when you say yes, I'll give it to you."

My knees went weak, and I had to lock them so he wouldn't know. Something was very wrong with me because that was so hot. Not that I would let on. "Did you just smell me?" I injected a note of disgust that I sure as shit didn't feel.

When he leaned back, I tensed at the sight of his grin. It was sexy and filled with all the promises his body was saying, but the animosity between us wouldn't let either of us do it. *Right?* "Knock it off." Confusion mixed with hatred. Not liking the shift between us, I shoved at him. "Let me go, or things are going to get difficult for you." I had my ace in the hole. "You think you've got something on me?" I leaned in, dropping my voice to a seductive purr. "I've got news for you."

I fished my phone from my back pocket and thumbed up the picture I'd taken of the bruise on my calf. "Bet the football team won't take kindly to the little souvenir their star tight end gave me."

His gaze narrowed, and he growled. Several seconds passed

as his hold intensified, and I felt his erection against my stomach. It ignited something inside me. How could I want him when he was such a colossal asshat? Heat pooled low. It was enough to make me angrier, and I put as much weight as possible behind my palms as I pushed him away.

He laughed, but I caught the edge to it. *That's right, asshole. I'm well versed in this game.*

But this time, he gave in. The hold on my hair lessened, and his arm fell away.

I scurried back, bumping into someone behind me. A startled "hey" sounded, but they must have gotten a look at Cole over my shoulder because nothing else was said or done. The power he and his group had over the other students was mind-blowing. And I'd caught his attention. None of it was good.

His features hardened. Gone was the raw lust from seconds ago. In its place was nothing but hate. I shivered for an entirely different reason.

"Go home," Cole sneered. "This isn't your crowd, anyway."

He might as well have thrown a bucket of cold water over me. My body cooled instantly. I stumbled back, the lumpy sand making it hard to execute a fast retreat. Gaining my footing, I turned, only to find a wall of girls a few feet away. Their expressions promised retribution.

Perfect. Just what I need, to be stalked by his fan club.

CHAPTER TEN

COLE

When Riley walked into a room, I got hard.

That was all she had to do. I wanted her out of my system.

It was the chase. Once I had her, I could get past it and drive her out of town. We were not letting her mother into our house. And as for Riley's little threat with that picture… it cancelled mine out, as far as I was concerned, and I had to admit that her fire fueled my own. It was an interesting little game of foreplay we had going on.

I scrubbed my hands over my face and stood. Breakfast then workout. We had off from practice—not because of the win. Our coaching staff had meetings or something like that. I didn't take days off, though. My goals didn't leave room for downtime.

The past two days flipped through my thoughts—nothing new. Riley was always on my mind. Thursday night's bonfire had been amusing. The only saving grace was the way Riley felt in my arms. The way she smelled, her softness, and that feisty temper kept me coming back for more—and that was in addition to the revenge I wanted against my dad. She was driving me crazy, turning into an obsession I had trouble kicking, and I'd welcomed the football game against HVH Friday night.

We'd dominated. I knew we would. Phoenix's arm was on fire as he threw one touchdown pass after another. We'd caught and run for seven touchdowns among my brother, Shane and me. It was a sweep. HVH hadn't stood a chance.

The stands had been packed with an intense crowd. I'd looked for her. A part of me had wanted her to be there, to watch me in action. She wanted me—that had been evident on Thursday when her eyes dilated and her lower lip trembled before she clamped her mouth shut.

Every inch of her was toned to perfection but soft in all the right places. I had to get her out of my system soon before I burst. Nothing helped. Not jerking off in the shower to her image—which was hot as hell, or getting someone else underneath me.

I didn't want anyone else.

I glanced at the clock right as it turned nine. I'd overslept, even though it was Saturday. I had enough time to get a run in before lifting with the guys. The fight was tonight, and I hoped it would curb some of the darkness in Damon. This shit with Dad was pushing him over the edge. For me, too, but I had to hold it together for him.

I would never forget finding Mom last summer, lying on her bed amidst empty pill bottles, her eyes sightless. Dad's affairs and neglect were to blame. The evidence of him being at that legal conference with another woman then coming home to find that Mom had died by suicide had broken Damon—and honestly, me. But that had been the nail in the coffin for Dad when it came to them. Prior to that, he had been more forgiving of our father's misdeeds.

I would not let our parents' actions destroy my brother. As it was, he needed fights or sex to stay sane.

I pounded on his door as I walked by on my way toward the kitchen. "Get up. We're running in five."

"Go to hell."

I laughed at the rough sound of his voice, backed up, then hit his door harder. "Come on, motherfucker. Get your ass out of bed."

I waited until I heard the thump of his feet hitting the floor. With that done, I lengthened my stride to grab a small glass of water and shoes. Today was leg day. Nobody liked leg day, but it was better than shoulders and chest, given the fight later. The five-mile run and sprints on the field before the fight could give our opponents a chance.

Probably not. Especially with Damon.

I was on the fence about continuing the fights. Getting caught was a huge risk that could end my goals. I kept going for the money. We didn't need it because we each had credit cards from Dad and our trust would kick in at twenty-one, but our cousins sure as shit did.

That was another point of contention with our dad. We'd approached him about setting up college funds for Phoenix and Shane, but he said that he bought them the cars and if they wanted to go to college, their father could pitch in, since he was making good money.

Their worthless dad did have money. He was in the NFL, which was where the drive behind Phoenix and Shane's desire to be the best came from. They were determined to get drafted and then prove to their father how much better they were than him—and tell the world that he had done nothing to help them get where they were.

Damon and I had wanted to help, so we started the fights. Our cousins weren't destitute, but Thane was a Division-I school with a hefty price tag. And even if they got a partial scholarship, they would have to come up with most if not all of the remaining balance, plus money for housing and food.

Our cousins stayed in a nice house with their mom. Their grandparents helped her pay the mortgage. She was an ER nurse, so she made decent money but not enough to live in our neighborhood, despite their house being the smallest one in it.

When I entered the kitchen, I flipped through my messages. There were pictures from the bonfire and too many messages to count from Piper. I deleted the stream without reading any. She was on her way to being blocked.

I grabbed a glass, filled it with water, and took a gulp, still reading my messages.

"You must be Damon."

A smokey, familiar voice shocked me, so I sucked some water down the wrong pipe. After a coughing fit, I turned in the voice's direction. She was at the breakfast table by the bay window overlooking the pool. I hadn't noticed her when I'd walked in.

The ice machine whirled, and she glanced briefly to the side. Everything in me froze, and I was transported—again—to that day last summer, Mom's note for Dad, and finding her lifeless body on her bed.

I forced myself to stay calm as I took in the woman's blond mane of hair. It was shorter, but if it had been dark brown, which I suspected was her natural color, it would have been identical to Riley's, as was the almond shape of her dark brown eyes, and her heart-shaped face. *How had I not recognized that Riley was demon spawned?*

I didn't answer her. All I could do was stare. Then Dad entered, dressed in dark-gray Armani pants and a thin cashmere sweater. "Oh good, you're here, Cole. Have you met Raelyn?"

"No." I'd never officially met her, but I recognized her and what she represented to our family. She was why my mom was dead.

"This is the woman I told you about." He glanced at his watch. She stood beside him, reading the cue, a soft smile on her deceptive lips. "Things have gotten rather serious between us. I'd hoped to tell you earlier, but time got away from me. Raelyn and her daughter are moving in, and we hoped we would go to lunch today so you and your brother can get to know them."

Rage filled me, and I knew I had to get away from them—from her—before I exploded. I brushed past, careful not to get too close on my way to where I'd left my running shoes. I bent and swiped them from the floor to put them on once outside. I couldn't get out of there quickly enough.

Christ, Riley looked just like her whore of a mother. I couldn't believe I hadn't put it together.

My Little Thief's mother was the woman who had been the ultimate nail in Mom's coffin. It changed everything. They were in my world and would pay for the destruction they'd caused.

I couldn't wait for my brother, who had probably gone back to sleep. I took off, not bothering to stretch. I took a sharp right to exit the backyard and headed for the beach. It would be fairly empty, and I could get lost in my thoughts as I ran, which was what I knew would happen.

I would never forget that bitch or the way Dad's hand touched her. The possessiveness in the way he'd done it told me everything I needed to know about the woman who'd managed to destroy our family.

That thought spiraled me into the past, with me standing at Mom's bedside.

"Take it, Cole." Mom extends her hand. Dad's name is scrawled on the envelope.

She hasn't gotten out of bed again. Dad hired a nurse to help her. I hate coming in here. Her room is dark and smells like when Damon and I have the flu. She's depressed, and there's nothing we can do to change it, no matter how hard we try. This is different. Whatever the envelope contains brought a spark back into her eyes. Not a good one, though.

"Dad's out of town this weekend. He'll be back on Monday."

"No." Her voice gains strength, and I see the fiery beauty she used to be before things between her and Dad went to hell. "It has to be today. Take your brother and go to the conference." She grabs my wrist and presses the letter into my hand. "Make sure you give it to him and no one else. Tell him to open it right there in front of you, or he'll just shove it into his pocket and forget about it. Promise me."

She's getting agitated, and I don't want to be the cause of another one of her episodes. "The nurse leaves in a couple of hours. I won't be back in time if you need something."

"Cole." She falls back onto her pillows, and that dullness that I've come to hate coats her eyes once more. "I'm a grown woman. If I need anything, I can get it for myself."

"Okay. Damon and I'll be back as soon as possible." I hate leaving her alone. The nurse is supposed to stay overnight when Dad's away, but she has a sick kid and can't, since her husband works nights. I can't blame her. It isn't our housekeeper's job either. Dad should have hired more people to help Mom. Mom refuses to take her meds, and this is what happens. Of course, Dad doesn't care enough. He never has.

My feet pounded on the packed sand, and gulls cried overhead. The rhythmic back-and-forth of the waves breaking just shy of my footfalls brought me back to the present and the problem at hand. I'd taken Damon to the conference that godawful day last year, and we'd found Dad. He hadn't been alone.

I took my phone off the strap that adhered it to my bicep and shot a text off in the group chat with Damon, Phoenix, and Shane: *Riley is mine. No one fucks with her but me.*

They knew to freeze her out, to keep any guy from dating her away, but everything was different now. I would go into details later. I didn't want to involve them in who she was until I had to. Damon was already struggling, and I worried this would put him over the edge.

Riley had no idea what she'd stepped into when she'd moved

here with her scheming mother. Everything changed that day last year when I delivered that note.

Riley's mom, Raelyn, had been the catalyst for my broken family and my brother's rage—for mine.

It was time to make her pay.

CHAPTER ELEVEN

RILEY

My phone vibrated again on the small side table next to the couch. The first time, I'd been able to ignore it. The second and third finally forced me to tear my eyes from the TV. I would have, anyway, since the movie was almost over and the sun had been streaming through the partially opened blinds. I'd forgotten to close them the night before.

I slapped my hand on the table until I found my phone. After unplugging the power cord, I squinted at the screen and pushed myself up. I dropped my feet to the floor and shut off the TV. Mom had texted an address and told me to go there when I was awake and showered. *Newsflash, Mom, I had a movie marathon last night, party of one.*

She'd been gone a solid week with no real explanation. And now, a summons.

I couldn't help but laugh. She was my mom, but she was also my best friend. Our relationship was unusual. Being on the run did strange things to people, and we had a bond that most other parents and children did not.

A week was too long. I couldn't wait to see her. But there was no way I would let her know how happy I was about it. She needed to grovel. She owed me. I threw back the covers, and my feet landed on the cool wooden floor before I hurried into the bathroom to shower.

It didn't take me long to get ready, although I wasn't leaving until I had a cup of coffee. Priorities. On second thought, picking up a to-go one from the coffee shop not far from the house sounded better. Purse in hand, I exited the house, locked the door, then got into my Charger. *Thank you, Uncle Ronan.* I seriously loved that car.

The line for the drive-through was long, but I got my coffee then punched in the address Mom had texted into my GPS. It was weird to be going in blind. Usually, when she wanted me to meet her somewhere, we had an entire plan and a loose script to follow to get the score we'd planned. I was still excited to see her, but this was strange.

It was bright and sunny, and I had the windows rolled down, which helped to dry my hair. It would be a bit messy, but Mom wouldn't care. I hoped she'd wrapped her mark up tight and nothing I did would hinder her progress. Because a week—she already had serious groundwork laid. A spark of annoyance burst in me. Yeah, she had some major groveling to do for not including me in her con.

The neighborhood changed from modest homes to sprawling estates, and by the time I pulled up to a gated community and was buzzed through, my jaw was on the ground. I followed the directions past homes that screamed wealth, finally turning onto a long driveway that led to a brick mansion complete with turrets and glimpses of the ocean as its backdrop. *Holy hell. Is this score going to be my college fund?* Lord knew we needed it—or I did, especially since I'd never joined the diving team to try for a scholarship.

I'd been to Phoenix's party in a similar neighborhood last year. But it had been at night. I doubted this was the same one.

Keep a low profile. That was what Mom had drilled into my

head for as long as I could remember. This would not be a low profile. I felt uneasy. And another weird thing was that she wanted me to go out for the diving team at school. I needed to have a conversation with her to find out why.

I pulled into the circular driveway then got out of my car and went up the handful of steps to the impressive front door. I rang the doorbell and then waited awkwardly. The door opened, and my body went rigid. I was unsure of what to expect. A woman wearing a uniform answered. The kind smile on her weathered face warmed her eyes, and I returned it with a genuine one.

"Hi." I tried to see behind her, but the only thing visible was a table holding a massive bouquet. A grand staircase curved along the back of the marble foyer housing a large chandelier centered above the table. "My mom asked that I meet her here." That sounded sketchy until I heard the unmistakable sound of Mom's laughter.

"Of course, dear." The older woman stepped back. "Come right in." She shut the door behind me. "They're in the kitchen. If you'll follow me."

As we walked from the front of the house to the back, I suddenly regretted wearing jean shorts and an off-the-shoulder sweatshirt that had seen better days. My gym shoes had a hole in them, and I had no idea what my hair looked like after I had driven with the windows down.

I took a deep breath and shoved all insecurities aside. This was temporary. Whatever impression I made on the owners of this place didn't matter. We would move before I got too comfortable here, like always. Light spilled into a large, white chef's kitchen with gleaming stainless-steel appliances and a fancy backsplash.

"Riley."

My mom's voice yanked my focus from a visual exploration of

the kitchen to where she stood with a tall, handsome man who had some graying at the temples of his jet-black hair. He looked like a silver fox, someone attractive and wealthy—another red flag that had me questioning what was up with her. I was used to portly wealthy men, not ones who could potentially steal her heart.

When I could tear my eyes from him, I sucked in a breath. She'd gone *Stepford*. Already gorgeous in a just rolled-out-of-bed way, this put-together version of herself was shocking. Seriously, Mom could wear a burlap sack and look fantastic. Her dark-brown hair was dyed blond, which wasn't surprising, since she loved to color it. We both did out of necessity. Diamonds—new ones, since I knew she didn't own anything like that—winked from her ears, and her hair was carefully tamed into a chignon. *What the hell? Is she wearing red lipstick?* The mom that I knew hated that color. She wore pretty shades of pink if anything at all.

She separated herself from the breakfast table, where she had a cup of coffee, our only drug of choice after the run-in she had with painkillers. That had been a tough month. Another person was at the table, but his back was to me. I looked back at the man standing at her side. Something was familiar about him, but I couldn't put my finger on it.

She stepped away from him then hugged me, which I returned as questions swirled in my head. Over her shoulder, the other guy at the table turned, and everything in me stilled. I barely stopped myself from cursing out loud. This was her new boyfriend's house, and I knew who was at the table.

When she pulled away, I shot her a glare that conveyed that we would be talking at the earliest moment. She winked. *Seriously, what the hell?*

"Riley." Chills skated down my spine as Damon—*or should I call him Demon?*—stood. "I don't think we've officially met. I'm Damon."

I know who the fuck you are, Demon. I masked my feelings of terror and gave him a smirk before turning my back on him.

"I'm glad you two have met." Her smile couldn't have been brighter, and she returned to the man's side. His arm automatically slipped around her waist, and she leaned into him. I wanted to gag. "Lucas's other son is around here somewhere."

I'm sure he is. Lying in wait to pounce was my bet. "Don't worry about it. We met at school." She knew as much. I narrowed my eyes at her, willing her to read how mad I was.

She didn't react. Not even a flinch. I could feel a headache coming on. An awkward silence fell between us, and I wanted to slap the gleeful look off Damon's smug face. That asshole was loving this. Lucas and I exchanged greetings before his phone rang, and he excused himself to answer it.

"We're going to lunch together."

"You and me?" I pressed my lips together—*get the message, Mom.* I would rather have eaten chalk than go anywhere with Cole and Damon.

"No, the five of us. We thought it would be a great way for you all to get to know each other a little better."

"Yeah, sorry." I backed away, ready to pivot and get the hell out of there. "I can't make it. I have that thing we talked about today."

"Riles."

I waved over my shoulder, already exiting the kitchen. "Sorry, Mom. Rain check." *More like never.* I made a beeline for the front door then yanked it open and rushed out, only to smack into a shirtless, sweaty chest—*Cole. Goddammit!*

CHAPTER TWELVE

COLE

Finished with my run, which helped shake a small amount of the anger, I reached for the door to go inside and shower. Only I didn't need to. Someone yanked it open. A flurry of dark hair and motion plowed into me. My hands automatically went to her shoulders to help steady the unfortunate person now covered in my sweat.

The scents of lilac and honey invaded my senses, as did the feeling of her body pressed against mine, and I knew at that moment who was in my space. My hands gripped her shoulders as she stepped back then looked up. Our eyes met.

I flashed her a smile that probably belied the wicked things I was thinking. "We've got to stop meeting like this."

She scowled then tensed, ready to jerk out of my hold. Instead, her mouth fell open with a gasp. Everything in me stilled as her fingers grazed underneath the bruise I had on my cheekbone from last night's fight. The electricity of her touch traveled straight to my dick, and I wanted to pull her close so she would know what her touch provoked. *Soon...*

But I was getting off track. I needed to stay focused on what I would do to her. Sleeping with her was a side bonus to get her out of my system for good. The rest would be geared to run her out of town. "I'm fine." I shifted enough that her touch fell away.

Her scowl returned, and something dark swam in her eyes. "If you don't ice that, you'll regret it."

Something about her tone froze everything in me. I didn't like it. "And how would you know about that?"

Some of the color drained from her face, and her eyes changed from alert to unfocused. *What is she remembering? Who the hell hurt her?* My grip tightened on her shoulders. The slight wince brought home how hard I held her, and I relaxed my fingers.

This was all wrong. I couldn't care. Not about her. Wanting her was one thing, but giving a shit about what she'd been through was another story. I refused to get involved. The change in my grip seemed to pull her from her thoughts, and she flicked her hair over her shoulder.

She took a deep breath and pasted a fake smile onto her face. "Whatever. I don't care what you do or look like." Her full lips curved into a wicked grin as she reached into her pocket then flashed me the picture of her calves—an accident I'd never meant to cause—from the damn bag slipping from my fingers and making a loud sound. "Only that you leave me alone."

I laughed at her blatant lie. I was about to call her out on it just as Raelyn's voice sounded from somewhere behind Riley. She was headed this way. The wall I'd erected where they were concerned slammed back into place. I never should have let it slip. Raelyn, I wanted to avoid, but Riley and I had unfinished business. "Our pictures cancel each other out," I said.

I released Riley's shoulders and grabbed her hand, yanking her to the stairs and avoiding everyone in the back of the house. She didn't say a word, and I guessed she wanted to avoid her mom, too, so I dragged her along until we reached my room on the second floor.

The whole way to my room, the softness of her skin drove

me crazy. Once inside my bedroom, I released her and shut the door behind me, moving farther within. Her eyes widened, and she whirled around in an attempt to leave. That couldn't happen. Before she could escape, I grabbed her hand and pulled her toward the bathroom. "Didn't you say I needed ice?"

She shook her head, making that thick, long hair sway. I wanted to fist it again and guide her to where I wanted her the most.

"It's cool." She tugged against my hold. "I'll go get you ice."

"There's ice over there." I pointed at the mini fridge in my room.

Her face paled. The more time I spent with her, which wasn't nearly enough, fed little clues about her personality. The only thing was, I didn't know what was real. Here, she acted like a scared little virgin. But in every other encounter, her fiery personality gave off a worldly vibe that screamed that she could take care of herself. I didn't know which was real or if it was a combination.

My cheek throbbed. It wasn't my first time dealing with the aftermath of a lucky punch. If I hadn't been distracted with thoughts of her, Landon never would have touched me. As it was, I'd knocked him out right after.

When she still didn't move, I gestured to the mini fridge, where I kept some ice packets. She rolled her eyes. I could tell she was holding in some smart-ass comment, making no effort to get one, as I moved around her then grabbed an ice pack. She was halfway between the bed, where I wanted her the most, and me. I let my gaze trail over every inch of her before slowly landing on her face then backed her toward my bed.

At the last second, she turned to avoid being pushed onto it. I wanted to grab her, but it wasn't time yet. We could draw it out, this insane sexual tension between us. And I was on board with the cat-and-mouse game we seemed to be playing.

"I have to go." The words rushed from her mouth as she backed away from me.

"Why are you fighting it?" I taunted. "You feel the chemistry too."

Sparks danced in her eyes. Goddamn, she drove me crazy. I wanted to close the distance between us to experience the full force of the heat from her anger.

"Sure." Her hand curled around the doorknob. "But I hate you."

"We have that in common." I moved before she could react and hauled her against me. One finger beneath her chin, I tilted her head back and spoke against her mouth. "Let's get it out of our system so we can hate each other without this thing between us."

She leaned in and placed her palm on my chest, and my pulse spiked. "That would be one way."

Her tongue darted out and traced her full bottom lip. More siren than anything else. The rest of the room faded. There was only Riley and what I salivated to taste.

She shoved me so that I took a step back in the direction of my bed, more than willing to go there so long as she followed.

"But this"—she gestured between us—"is never gonna happen."

With that, she whipped open the door, lurched into the hallway, and disappeared from view as she raced to the stairs. Dark laughter filled my room before I realized it was coming from me. This was way more fun than it was supposed to be.

One thing was certain. She wanted me. I could tell from how the pulse at the base of her neck beat furiously and how her pupils dilated whenever we touched. I would use that to lure her in and ruin her completely—which would be a solid way to hurt her mother.

CHAPTER THIRTEEN

RILEY

That asshole.

I slammed the door to my car, stormed over to the button to close the garage, then went inside, fuming the entire way. I had been off-balance from the moment I arrived at Cole's house. And it wasn't a house. It was a freaking mansion. Who lived like that? I grimaced. Apparently, they did.

At the sink in the kitchen, I turned on the water and scrubbed my hands with soap, trying to get the feeling of his sweaty, muscular chest off them. Bending over the sink, I splashed water on my heated face. He affected me way too much. I could never let him know. *What's wrong with me?* It wasn't like I hadn't come across jerks like him, the dicks who ran whatever temporary school I was at. Top-tier asshole athletes who thought they were better than everyone else were everywhere. Predictable. Untouchable.

But he wasn't either of those things, and the way his body had tensed with hard muscles that bulged and shifted under my touch was confirmation. With a decisive push, I shut off the water, grabbed a towel, and dried my hands and face as the truth of what had happened resonated deep inside me—I affected him. A slow grin formed, and a spark of glee followed. *Wonder how that made him feel.*

Leaning a hip against the counter, I couldn't help but wonder if that was why he propositioned me to have sex with him. Maybe "getting it out of our systems" was really his inability to deny how much he wanted me. I laughed loudly, loving that I'd gotten under his skin so badly. It made the fact that he was under mine a bit more bearable.

I wasn't going to give in to him. He was the same asshole as ever, even though he seemed single-minded when he touched me and tried to convince me to sleep with him. I shifted to break free from the heat he'd ignited with his touch. Even if I did give in, he'd screw with me in some other way to get a rise out of me. Worse, it would be personal because he would've had access to all of me. Not my mind, but sex changed things enough that his barbs would go deeper.

That settled it. Two could play this game.

I pushed off the counter and headed to my temporary room. I had homework to do, and I was convinced more than ever that this was a sick game to him. No matter how he made me feel, I melted inside with a simple touch. He was toying with me, and I could not trust him.

I reluctantly grabbed my backpack from the corner and hefted it onto my bed. After riffling through the contents, I faced the fact that I had to write a rough draft for English and do about ten calculus problems. Between the two, I went with math, which was just easier. The rough draft required my nonresponsive brain cells to work. I was too preoccupied with what went down at Cole's house... and with Mom.

Time crawled by. The work was agonizing—not difficult but hard to focus on. I dropped my head to the paper. At least I was doing math old-school and not on my laptop. Or else the keyboard would mess everything up even more than my screwed-up world could handle, and I didn't want to redo what

I'd managed to finish. *This is useless.* Groaning, I slapped my hand against the paper, frustrated.

Why did Mom think she could fit into that world? We couldn't fit anywhere except together—it was what she always said. And I was the sucker who'd believed her. Look where that got me. In a rental by myself while she tried to, what, make a new life for herself? Where did I fit into that?

I couldn't take it anymore and grabbed my phone, shooting off a text to her, asking why she was over when we had this house. Nothing made sense anymore.

Screw it. I pulled up Cassie's contact then sent her a message to see if she wanted to do some retail therapy. God knew I needed it. It was that or break into the school and hit the pool, but I didn't think it would be empty on a Saturday.

She responded immediately, and we made plans to meet at the beach, where we could do some outdoor shopping at the boutiques not far from the boardwalk then spend a few hours suntanning. I wasn't one to turn down beach time and hurried to throw on a black bikini and a pair of jean shorts. After tossing a towel and sunscreen in my oversized bag, I donned my sunglasses and headed out.

The sun was shining, and I rolled my windows down, letting the warm air in. Everyone and their brother were out, and traffic crawled. Half an hour later, I arrived and found a parking space by sheer luck. Someone was leaving when I was about to pass. I almost got rear-ended for stopping short, but I got the spot. After paying to park for the next couple of hours through an app, I crossed the small stretch of sand to the boardwalk in search of Cassie, my flip-flops happily clapping along.

I inhaled the salt-laden air, my mood already improving. Contrary to where I was born—New York—I was a beach girl at heart. Being so close to the water melted the anger and frustration away, replacing them with a sense of contentment that brought a smile to my face. It didn't take long until I spotted

Cassie. She wore a white bikini and pink wrap with matching flip-flops. A huge grin stretched across her pretty face when she saw me.

I laughed, my gaze going right to the two to-go cups in her hand. "Whatcha got there?"

"Hey." Cassie passed one to me. "I thought this would be fun for the beach, so I raided my mom's stash."

I gave my cup the sniff test. "Whoa, you're not messing around." Vodka with a splash of OJ.

"Yeah, well"—her brows furrowed—"with your distress call of retail shopping, I guessed you were having a similar day to me."

She looked to the sky before leveling me with a face devoid of all happiness. "I slept with someone last night after swearing I never would again."

"Again, huh?" I took a small sip and cringed at the lethal combination. "You're going to have to share."

"Let's forgo the shopping and find a spot on the beach instead." Cassie pivoted without waiting for my response, so I followed.

"This sounds serious. Were feelings involved, or is the guy a class-A douche?"

"Both? Here"—she thrust her cup into my empty hand—"hold this."

Her shoulder bag, similar to mine, hit the sand hard, and she pulled out a towel and spread it out before taking both cups from me so I could do the same. Once we were situated, I shifted to my side to see her expressions and sip my drink. I would have to eat something and wait long enough for the alcohol to get out of my system before driving.

Cassie tossed me a sandwich wrapped in cellophane. "In case you're hungry. I didn't have time for breakfast." She unwrapped hers and took a large bite.

I did the same. After chewing and washing it down with

another sip, I got right to the point. "You need to spill. You can't drop something like that on me and then say nothing. Who was it, and why were there feelings involved? On your end, or his?"

She groaned and took a long pull from her cup. "You know how I warned you away from Hidden Valley's Elite?"

"Yeah." I didn't like where this was going. "Are you talking about Cole?"

"Worse. Damon."

"No, you didn't." A sense of relief hit me that I would unpack later. Instead, I grinned, enjoying her discomfort more than I should. "Tell me it was at least good."

A kid shrieked and ran near my towel, chased by another. Small granules of sand pelted my calf, which I brushed away absentmindedly. The mom wasn't far behind, apologies spilling from her mouth that we both reassured her weren't needed. It was a beach and bound to happen. When they were out of earshot, Cassie leaned close.

"I don't know why I couldn't resist him. I went to the fight. You know the one I invited you to, and you completely blew me off?"

"Hey, I didn't blow you off. I said no."

"Whatever." She rolled her eyes. "I was close to the ring when Damon went in. We made eye contact. That guy has those smoldering eyes. Bedroom ones that I swear make girls' panties spontaneously combust."

"That's an unusual analogy."

She smacked my arm. "Shut it. You know what I mean."

The corners of my lips twitched. Then the thing I ran from this morning popped into my mind—the feeling of Cole's sinfully bare chest under my fingertips. Sadly, I did get what she meant. "Okay, go on."

"As I was saying before you rudely interrupted me."

"Yeah, yeah." She was seriously cracking me up, which was

why I'd texted her to get together today. She was good people. I was lucky our paths had crossed that first day.

"He's animalistic when fighting. All fury and aggression. The way he animates his opponents is scarily hot."

"You get off on watching him beat the hell out of someone? I mean, no judgment here. I'm just clarifying."

"You would've, too, if you'd been there." Her voice took on a dreamy quality. "Then after, he wrapped his arm around my waist and pulled me against his side." She raised a shoulder then let it drop. "My brain shut off, and I just went. There wasn't even a tiny part of me that could reason my way out of why it was a bad idea."

"The sex was good?"

"Ahh, yeah. If you haven't had sex with one of the Elite, I would highly recommend it at least once. It's back-against-the-wall, all-consuming, you'll-never-forget-it kind of sex. My body is one big throbbing mess. It's like I can still feel him pounding into me repeatedly. Everything is hypersensitive. Even my clothes are turning me on."

"You're making me very uncomfortable here, Cass." But I was laughing. That sounded like one hell of a night.

She grunted then took another drink. "And that's why I brought drinks. I needed to dull my senses just a little, so I don't go to his house and pound on the door for another round... or four. But I'm not because he's not good for me."

"Why not? If you guys have a connection, maybe see where it goes?"

"For the same reason I warned you to be careful around them. Damon doesn't often sleep with the same girl twice."

I softened my voice because it felt like we were on emotionally charged ground with this part. "But he did with you, right?"

"Let me repeat this: he's not good for me, Riles. The sex is fantastic, but he'll rip my heart out without a second thought. The right guy for me isn't one of the Elite. I've known them all my life, and whenever we've interacted, bad things tend to happen."

"Are you talking about their fan club?"

"Yeah, Piper and her following. They don't share well, and they consider those four guys theirs. But that's not the only downside. Damon won't ever love me as I could him. And..." She worried her lip. "There's someone else I've liked for years."

"Then you should go for it with the other guy. Who knows," I teased. "The sex might be just as hot with him."

"Oh, I'm counting on it." Cass fanned her heated cheeks.

"So, who is he?"

"You know Matt Chambers from lit class?"

Cass and I had lit together. "I can't place him."

"He sits in the back, looks like he lives on the beach. Total surfer vibe."

"Oh, yeah." He had dirty blond hair and a perpetual laid-back attitude. Easy-breezy kind of guy that wasn't hard on the eyes either. "He's pretty hot. What's stopping you?"

"I'm not sure he's even aware of me on a relationship level."

I took in her toned body, which had just enough curves to make a guy stop and take notice. Add her blue eyes and cute pixie face, and I couldn't see anyone not noticing her. "That's crazy. He's aware. But you may be right about Damon being a problem. I doubt any guy in that stupid school would cross one of the Elite. I bet he wouldn't make a move if he thought you guys had something going on. So it's up to you to do something about it if you want the guy."

I had plenty of experience with that. I was a con's daughter. It was usually her snagging some mark, but I was fully aware of her process. And I didn't think Cassie would have to do more than put herself in the right place and speak a handful of words to him.

"Do you surf?"

"Of course. Who doesn't in this town?"

Point taken. We spent the next hour strategizing what she would do and where she would run into him—no surprise, it would be at the beach. And not this weekend but next, so the Damon encounter wasn't as fresh, since she was sure Matt would have heard about it.

"Thanks, Riles." The tension left her shoulders, and she looked lighter. "I'm so glad we met."

"Me too." I just hoped we could stay in town for a while. Aside from the nightmare encounters I had with Cole, I genuinely liked Cassie. And not that I would admit it, but she was my first real friend. We'd moved around too much for me to make any that stuck before. It would be nice if for once, I could have one. Maybe even finish out the year here.

We swapped our drinks out for water that she magically pulled from her bag. I usually had one in mine but had been in such a hurry to get out of the house I'd forgotten to pack some.

"We've spent this entire time talking about me. It's your turn." She shoved a handful of hair behind her ears that the wind had blown in her face. "Spill."

I'd never talked about anything Mom and I were involved in, but since she wasn't talking to me... I needed to vent. "My mom's dating someone."

"Okay. And that's a problem why?"

"Because it's Lucas Savage."

"Holy shit!"

Water pelted me as Cassie jolted into a sitting position. "Hey!" I lightly dabbed under my eyes.

"Sorry." She swiveled so she was on her knees and leaning toward me. "Your mom is dating Damon and Cole's dad. I've got that right?"

"Unfortunately." I glanced warily at her. "You'll keep this quiet?"

"Oh, yeah. This can't get out. The bitch squad will be all over you and not in a good way."

"Lovely." I could handle them. But handling Cole was becoming increasingly problematic.

"How serious is it? Is it, like, a stepsibling situation?"

"Ew." I frowned at her. "That's just gross. And I doubt it. But it's weird. My mom and I are pretty close, since it's just us. But she's been spending so much time with him that everything's different."

"That sucks, but if there's one thing I know, it's that you've got to make sure Cole and especially Damon, since he's the wildcard, keep their mouths shut about it at school."

"And that's a big part of the problem. Cole's intent on making my life a living hell. I'm sure Damon will do his part too."

"And their cousins. Crap. Is there anything I can do?"

It took me a minute before I could respond. I wasn't used to anyone other than Mom or Uncle Ronan helping me, and her concern hit me hard, tightening my throat for a moment. "Thanks. I appreciate it, but I've got this." And I did. I'd handled worse. I just needed to get my head straight and make Cole my bitch.

Cassie and I hung out for another hour, enjoying the day, swimming, and chatting about random stuff. When it was time for her to go so she could watch her younger sister while her parents went out to dinner, I packed up too. I doubted Mom was back. It would be an empty home for me—*it had better be.* Cole needed to stay the hell out of there.

We walked to the parking lot together. It had turned out to be one of the best days I'd had in a long time. Cass leaned in and hugged me.

"It's been real," she said before releasing me and crossing to where she'd parked. Before she got in, she shouted over her shoulder, "Next time, we're going to the cove, where there aren't so many people."

"Sure. Later, Cass." The cove sounded interesting, and I

strangely longed for it to be next time. I wasn't looking forward to that empty house.

Back in the car, I took my phone out of my bag and stared at it. No texts. No missed calls. I didn't like it. Mom always checked in with me. I let it fester as I drove home. When I parked in the garage, I was done. Unable to stand it any longer, I shot off a text: *Why are you over there if you forced me to move into this other place?*

Not even a second passed before her text came in: *I'm going to fix that soon enough.*

I had no idea what she meant, but I knew I didn't like the ideas her cryptic response conjured and hit her contact button to call her. When she picked up, there was some shuffling then the quiet snick of a door closing.

"Riles? Everything okay?" Her voice was hushed.

Anger shot through me. "Why are you whispering? Don't want your mark to hear anything? You know, the con you *still* haven't let me in on?"

"Stop. I already explained, as did your uncle, that this isn't a con. I care for Lucas, and if you had bothered to go to lunch with us as I'd asked, you would have found out with his sons that he asked me to move in with him."

"Are you fucking kidding me?"

"I know that it's sudden."

"Sudden? When the hell did you meet this guy? A week ago?"

"About that… there's a lot I need to share with you. I'm coming home tonight, and we can talk then."

I hung up, too upset about everything. *Marriage? Huh.* I huffed out a breath. A part of me wanted to laugh when I wondered what Cole's reaction had been. A text came through as I turned on the shower to wash the beach off me.

Cassie: *Another fight tonight! It's at midnight. I'll pick you up. I need you to keep my head straight if Damon even glances in my direction. Don't bring your phone. They check them at the door.*

Oh, I would definitely bring my phone. I shot off a reply that I would see her there. The night just got infinitely better, or so I hoped. Unease danced along my spine. I knew I might have the same problem watching Cole fight as she had the other night with Damon.

Already, I pictured him, powerful and shirtless, his muscles bunching and rippling as he moved. I closed my eyes, but that made it worse. He was there. Over me, under me—freaking everywhere.

My knees went weak, and my breath came in short pants.

Yep, I was in for a world of trouble tonight.

CHAPTER FOURTEEN

COLE

"You sure about this?" Phoenix dropped his bag at his feet, surveying the crowd as if he hadn't asked me a loaded question.

The place was shoulder to shoulder, with half the academy's student body pumped up and placing bets. I nodded to Snake, a fellow senior and a rough linebacker whose appearance fit his nickname. He ran the fights and collected the money. He also made sure we got our payouts. No one crossed him without getting a beatdown. It'd happened once, and word got around.

"About what? The fight?" We were in an old standalone fieldhouse that the academy mainly used for yard equipment storage. It was the perfect place to hold fights.

The timing couldn't have been better. Damon got the word out. And a few hours later, we were inside.

"About Riley."

That got my attention. A glance told me that Shane and Damon were near the ring, talking to Tracey and a few girls who liked to hang around us. Piper tried to catch my eye, but I turned my back, not wanting to deal with her brand of crazy. I let the hype around me fade enough to focus solely on my cousin. His silver eyes bore into mine. "What are you talking about?"

"I stopped by earlier. You were out, but Damon told me that Riley lived with her mom only. And that you're making it your mission to intimidate her. She's a single mom, and that's her only kid." He crossed his arms over his chest, and a spark of annoyance ignited in my chest. "I don't know what's going on with you and that girl, but I saw you with her at the bonfire, and you're taking things pretty far, and you've involved us in it. We've never gone after a girl before. We leave that to them." He tipped his head in the direction of Piper and her entourage. "You need to explain."

"This isn't similar to your situation." I jabbed my finger into his chest. "You need to have my back like I always have yours."

A flash of guilt shot through his mercurial gaze. "I do. But what you're doing with her, the intimidation, it doesn't add up. Especially if things progress between your dad and her mom." He held up his hands when I growled. "I'm just saying I need to know more to keep freezing her out the way we are."

"Yet my brother doesn't question my motives."

Phoenix glanced at Damon. "Yeah, that's not surprising. His head has been all over the place even more than normal."

Fuck. He wasn't kidding. I was worried too. Damon was a loose cannon. The fights usually kept him reined in, but lately, not much worked. Our mom's death had messed him up. "I think Dad's new devotion to Riley's mom has gotten under his skin. It's stirring up memories."

"It's only been a year since Aunt Linda died. I get that it might seem too soon for your dad to move on."

"My dad fucking killed her. Of course, it's too soon, which is why Damon is a headcase."

The door to the field house opened, and I caught sight of several unfamiliar faces. A few guys had reached out and wanted to set something up last-minute. It had to have been them. The guys entering were from a few towns over, where one of the rougher, low-income high schools was. Our school wasn't in their division, but there were rumors, none of them good, about a few of their players.

"Damon," I called then waited until he disengaged from Jessica, one of the cheerleaders in our orbit. When he joined us, I pointed out the biggest of the guys we were fighting. "You've got him."

"Shit, that guy has to be six four."

I caught Phoenix's eyes and grinned because my brother's words didn't match the sheer determination and menace tightening his features. Size didn't matter. Rage and skill did. And my brother had both in spades. It made him a machine on the football field and one of the best defensive ends in the state.

A wave of unfamiliar faces followed the fighters who neared the makeshift ring. The place was packed, which meant we had little time to waste if we didn't want an unexpected visit from the cops. Phoenix approached Snake to set things in motion.

While Snake took the center of the mats we used as our ring, I scanned the crowd. An unsettling awareness danced over my skin that could only have meant one thing: she was here somewhere. Every muscle in my body was strung tight. The feeling of her stayed with me. No matter what I did, I couldn't get her out of my mind, which was why I'd so readily agreed to the fight tonight.

Without catching sight of Riley, I pushed her to the back of my mind. I didn't have to like her to sleep with her. And that was what I would do. But I needed to take my aggression out on my opponent. I nodded to Snake, letting him know I wanted to go next. I didn't care who I took on. They would lose, just like the big guy would against my brother. We would make bank on that fight too. The guy had three inches on Damon and at least a hundred pounds.

And the more money we made on the fight, the more we

could put into the account for Phoenix and Shane to go to college.

Snake stuck two fingers in his mouth and whistled. The crowd settled, and a dark grin spread across his mouth. "We all know what we're here for, so let's cut the bullshit, skip the rules, and get to it!"

I shook my head in amusement as Snake introduced Drake, the behemoth, and Damon as the night's first round. Both were packed with muscle, but whereas Damon had little to no body fat, Drake had a noticeable belly. Typical of defensive guards, which I had no doubt he was.

Snake rang the bell, and Damon and Drake circled, sizing each other up. I knew when my brother would strike before he even moved. He delivered quick jabs packed with power then danced out of reach. Drake's arm span was longer, but Damon was lightning fast with limitless endurance. They traded punches, Drake landing half the number that Damon did, though his were just as powerfully delivered.

"It's coming," I warned Phoenix, and we moved closer as one unit. We know how Damon would react once he got the guy on the ground. He would pulverize him until there was nothing left. The haze of the fight wouldn't lift fast enough.

Then it happened: one punch to Drake's jaw, and his eyes rolled back in his head. He wavered on his feet, and Damon delivered another. The power of it sent him back to land on the mat with a resounding thud. Cheers went up. The crowd was pumped. Damon jumped on Drake, his elbow cocked back to deliver punishing blows. I grabbed the crook of his arm, locking mine through his and pulling him back as Phoenix did the same. We wrestled him away. "Enough."

It took another second for the word to penetrate. We didn't release him until the tension eased from his body.

"You good?" Phoenix asked.

Damon grunted. It was enough. We released him and

stepped back. Snake took our place and lifted Damon's fist over his head. "And the winner by knockout is our very own Demon!"

My brother's nickname fit because he was more demon than man in the ring.

Our rivals dragged Drake off the mat before I stepped up, opposite to a guy Snake announced as Mike. We were evenly matched, both slightly over six feet tall and with similar body types. Anger snapped in Mike's eyes, and I flashed him a wicked grin. He must not have liked what had happened to his buddy. I bet he wouldn't enjoy what came next.

Snake gave the signal, and I rushed my opponent, hitting him with a right hook then a left then dancing out of reach. He blocked the next one, and I waited for him to strike to read his tells. His weight shifted half a second before an aggressive combination of punches pounded into me. I blocked two, but the third struck home, splitting my lip.

We traded hits, mixing them up with combinations. It didn't take long to read him and to outmaneuver him, getting just out of reach. I let a few more hits find their marks, since they wouldn't impact me much. Soon, he wasn't holding his arms as high. His endurance and confidence took a beating. I used my quickness as an advantage, attacking with an uppercut in the sweet spot along his jaw. He swayed then sank to the ground, and I struck until Snake called the fight.

I stepped down, and that was when I saw Riley dressed in a fitted black T-shirt and ripped jeans. My fingers twitched with the need to feel her curves under me. Her long brown hair fell in waves around her ashen face. Full lips tempted me, and I couldn't fight the attraction.

I tapped Damon on the back. "I'm out. Make sure Phoenix and Shane are good."

He noted the lust in the look I gave her and laughed. "I got ya, bro. Have a nice ride."

Fucker. I moved forward, and people parted for me. Riley had pivoted and headed toward the exit, but my legs were longer. I caught up to her then grabbed her arm, my fingers curling tightly around her bicep. She glared as I forced her to turn. "Stepsister."

"Fuck you." Disgust added color back to her face.

"Leaving so soon?"

"I've seen enough."

She spat the words, but I caught the worry barely concealed in her features as her eyes fell to where my lip was split. Then she looked over my shoulder for a second too long. I did the same and found Matt Chambers in her line of sight. A wave of possession heated my blood, further fueling the adrenaline already coursing through me from the fight, and I knew we had to leave right away before I went over and beat Matt to a bloody pulp just because she'd looked at him.

I tightened my grip until she winced.

Easing up, I pulled her close, intent on hauling her out of there.

CHAPTER FIFTEEN

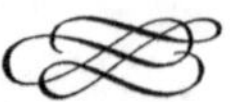

RILEY

"Get off me." I narrowed my eyes, every inch of me straining against Cole. It had been a mistake to come, and my body battled its core fight-or-flight instinct hard. His tight grip on my upper arm didn't help.

The only saving grace was that I'd told Cassie I was heading out and had pushed her in the direction of Matt, the guy she liked, who'd come in late. It was an opportunity she shouldn't pass up, which I told her.

My mind frantically weighed the odds of what could happen against the jerk hijacking my escape.

If Cassie saw that Cole had his meaty paws on me, everything would be ruined. She would come over to help. Damon would, too, if he noticed her getting involved, and I couldn't take a chance on that happening, not when she was interested in Matt. Damon would only see another guy as a challenge, since he'd hooked up with Cass recently. I couldn't be the one to sabotage her chances with someone else. Instead, I let the asshole manhandle me out of their makeshift venue.

I took one final glance over my shoulder as the meathead dragged me through the crowd, which magically parted for him like he was a god, reassuring me that Cassie hadn't noticed. But Piper had, and I knew that bitch would work even harder to make my life hell in school on Monday. The snide comments and shoulder checks that she'd been doing were child's play. She was going to escalate. I would need to do something about her and soon.

Cole gave me a hard yank, and I jerked forward. He pulled us through a door I hadn't noticed when I'd first gotten here. He reached behind me, and I heard the click of a lock before light flooded the small space. We were in some kind of locker room that must have been for the lawn maintenance staff. No one else was there, allowing me to get a grip on my emotions.

He jerked me to the left, slamming my back against the lockers. Anger flooded through me. I couldn't see straight. Pinned against the cold metal, I kicked out. He shifted, but my foot hit the side of his leg. It was enough to gain a few inches. Freedom was so close, and I bucked against him, but he grabbed me then pressed the length of his body over mine, effectively stopping any escape.

"You came to see me fight?"

His sinister smile further aggravated his split lip. I couldn't stop looking at it. A tiny degree of my anger cooled. I'd seen enough of those on Uncle Ronan, when he would stumble into our minuscule New York studio apartment. I'd been very young then, but it had left a big impression. "You should put something on that."

He didn't say a word, only stared at my lips. I was all too aware of his hardening body, and a spark of fear spliced through me. He wouldn't force himself on me, would he? Instantly, I cataloged anything around us that I could use as a weapon and calculated how quickly I could get to the door if I disabled him.

I was distracted. It was stupid. And I wasn't prepared when his lips crashed down on mine.

He devoured my mouth, sending jolts of desire through my

heated body. Everything faded—my anger, my need to run, and where we were. I existed only to feel. At the moment, there were only the two of us and our vulnerability and lust. Gone were the petty fights and unpredictable behaviors. He stripped my defenses away as his tongue danced with mine. Something primitive inside of me answered his call, and I wrapped my arms around his neck, tangling my fingers in his hair and tugging to bring him impossibly closer.

A deep, wanton moan slipped past my lips, swallowed by his mouth. But it was enough of a shock to remind me that our actions would lead to inevitable pain and sorrow. That small sliver of reality broke the haze he'd created with one touch, and I shifted my hands, trailed my palms down his chest until I had the best leverage, then shoved hard, catching him off guard. He stumbled back a step, his hold on me loose enough for me to break free. I'd already seen how unnaturally quickly he moved in the fight and couldn't waste my one chance at freedom. I leaped to the side, grabbed the doorknob, unlocked it with a flick of my finger, then used all my strength to yank it open and lunge out of there.

The crowd was thick and teeming with lust and violence. No one noticed me as another cheer went up for whatever had happened in the ring. Without a backward glance for fear that Cole was on my heels, I sprinted toward the exit and into the night. The fight had been insane, a first for me in terms of organized high school underground betting. My car wasn't far, and I ran full out, not stopping until I was behind the wheel. I roared out of there, my phone with the short video of Cole's fight tucked safely in my bra.

My lips tingled and burned as I sped down the road toward home. The faint metallic taste of his blood from the cut on his mouth lingered. That had been the most erotic kiss I'd ever experienced. I pressed two fingers against my still-tingling lips and knew everything had changed.

What did I just do?

CHAPTER SIXTEEN

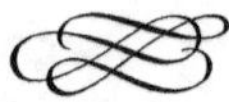

COLE

"That's not going to help." Damon tapped the back of his knuckle against the frozen peas pressed to Shane's cheek. "You're already ugly."

Shane chucked them at my brother. "Shut up, fucker. And how'd you barely get a mark on you?"

"Skill." Damon winked. "I've got it. You lack it."

"You're both idiots." Phoenix passed Shane a game controller.

I grunted in agreement. Done playing, I got up and headed to the wet bar to grab two more beers from the fridge. We kept the basement kitchenette fully stocked. Dad rarely came down here, and Mom never had. It was our domain. Our cousins had crashed at our place. Their mom worked nights, so it wouldn't have been a big deal if they'd gone home after the fight, but I knew Phoenix wanted information.

"I've waited long enough. Spill." One thing I could always count on from Phoenix was that he didn't mess around. He wouldn't let me off the hook about my reason for hating Riley.

I handed him a beer. We were on the couch opposite where Shane and Damon were engaged in a heated round of *Grand*

Theft Auto. I twisted off the top and tossed it onto the table before taking a long pull and dealing with his expectant expression. "Her mom is dating our dad."

"Well, fuck." Shane laughed. "Was that so hard to share with the class?"

"There's more, dickhead." I threw a pillow at his head. A volley of cussing occurred on the other couch after Shane's player crashed and burned. Damon didn't say a word. Unusual. I'd have to revisit that after our cousins were gone.

"Doesn't sound like there's more. Sounds like a classic scare-the-moochers-so-your-dad-doesn't-get-what-he-wants move."

"Replacement Mom isn't an option," Damon growled. And my brother was back, lousy mood and all.

"We met her yesterday."

"Makes sense about the fight." Phoenix knew us well. "What's she like?"

"Raelyn?"

"That's her name?" Phoenix grinned. "Doesn't sound like much of a threat."

"And that's the wrong assumption." Meeting her stuck in my head in a bad way but oddly, not as much as Riley's impact. That kiss. I couldn't get her taste or the sexy little moan out of my mind. No matter how badly I treated her, I only wanted more.

"So…" This from Shane.

"Raelyn gave me the impression she was a lot like Riley. Feisty as hell and too smart for her own good. She's gorgeous and already has our dad wrapped around her finger."

"What's the big deal if he sticks with this one? You're out of here after this year."

"What the fuck?" Damon groused. "I've got another year, just like you two assholes. And the last thing I want is someone playing mother dearest while making our undeserving father happy."

"I don't know, man. It just seems weak. Riley's a senior too."

"And if your dad came back to town?" I posed the question to Phoenix, who didn't seem to fully understand my motivation behind wanting to scare Riley and her mom away. "Possibly with a wife and kid?"

"Fine." Phoenix's easygoing expression turned murderous. He slammed the beer down on the table, and a few droplets sprayed out and landed on the smooth surface. When he stood, his hand met the back of his brother's head as he passed by. "Come on, Shane. We need to go."

Shane glared at me as he tossed the controller down then followed. Silence weighed heavily between Damon and me as he finished his round and shut the game off.

"That was low."

"Yeah, but I'm tired of them questioning me. Freeze her out. It's not too much to ask."

Damon met my gaze and held it for a long, uncomfortable minute, and I worried he saw too much. "Riley's not that bad. You want to go after someone? Let's take on the mom."

With that parting statement, Damon pushed off the couch and left too.

My head fell into my hands, and I scrubbed my palms over my face before getting up and heading upstairs. He had a point, but it was Riley that drove me nuts, and I had a feeling that if I made her life hell, it would affect her mom. Especially with how her mom had gushed about her daughter at lunch. She loved her, like, lots. Her face lit up, and she'd bragged about her enough that it made Damon and me uncomfortable. She displayed a kind of purity and devotion that we'd never experienced from either of our parents.

I hardened my thoughts. This was about revenge against my dad, and I planned to use her kid to orchestrate it. Distracted, I failed to notice my dad when I walked into the kitchen until it was too late. He was at the table, eating a sandwich, when I opened the fridge to take out leftovers.

"What did you think of Raelyn?"

I ducked into the fridge to hide the rage I felt. Once I regained enough control to put on the mask I needed to wear around him and didn't find the leftovers, I pulled out the cold cuts and bread. I would have a better chance of driving them away and ruining the relationship—like he destroyed Mom—if he didn't know how I felt. I could fake it for the time being.

"I only met her yesterday, so I don't think anything yet."

He narrowed his eyes, studying me. Ignoring him, I took out two pieces of bread, several pieces of sandwich meat, and a tomato then put them all together, adding mayo before sitting at the table opposite him as if I had nothing to hide. I ate in silence as he continued to watch me. *Good luck detecting anything, old man.* I'd played that game with him before and won.

"I want Raelyn and her daughter to feel welcome here."

Okay, I'll bite. "Why's that?" I took a large mouthful then raised my gaze to meet his. He had the same bone structure as me, same body shape. But I had Mom's green eyes and black hair to his brown-and-blue combo. It had to bother him to see parts of her in Damon and me when he looked at us. *Drown in it, asshole.*

"Because I haven't just asked her to move in. I also asked her to marry me."

Shit. I almost choked as I swallowed. *Marriage? Already?* I grabbed my water and chugged half of it. "That's pretty soon. Didn't you just meet each other?" *More like last year, right before Mom died.*

"I've known her casually for a while now. She worked at one of my other firms." He popped the last bite of his food into his mouth, chewed, then swallowed. "So what do you think?"

"Whatever, Dad." I got up, grabbed my empty plate and glass, and went to the sink. "Do what you want. You always do, anyway." I couldn't get out of there fast enough, but I forced the rage down and left the room at a normal pace.

Even as I stormed up the stairs and to my room, the thought of them moving in rolled around my head. As much as I hated the idea of it, there was an upside.

Riley would be at my mercy, day and night.

CHAPTER SEVENTEEN

RILEY

"I'm sorry."

I tossed my phone, not wanting to deal with another apology from Mom for breaking our plans. She had been a no-show last night. She'd called and apologized for having to break our plans.

"Your mom again?" Cass asked.

"Yep." I popped the *P*. "Lucas surprised her with tickets to some show in the city, and they decided to stay overnight."

I felt like my relationship with her was slipping away. She was my best friend and should have been there to listen to me and bitch about what a jerk Cole was. She gave incredible advice, and if I ever needed it, it was the time.

I was so over it. It sucked, especially since Cole had kissed me that way, and I didn't know how to process it. So I broke down and texted Cassie, and she came over right away.

Having a friend had its perks. *Take that, Mom.*

We were hanging out in my room—not that we needed to be in there, since no one was home—but it was a normal thing to do.

Even though I had to vent about him, it felt strange to do it with anyone other than Mom. Another wave of anger swept through me. But she'd chosen her new boyfriend over me, so whatever.

Cassie pulled her brown hair into a loose topknot and then flopped onto my bed. "I've been going on about Matt and our maybe date."

I grinned. "What do you mean, 'maybe date'? The guy asked you to go surfing with him on Saturday. There's no maybe about it."

She rolled her eyes. "As I was saying, I've been talking about my stuff, but you haven't uttered one word about why you need to vent. What happened between you leaving the fight last night and this morning?"

I slapped her legs aside then sat on the bed and scooted back so I could lean against the headboard. It was a big bed to have all to myself. I'd only ever slept in a single unless I had to share a full or queen with Mom in whatever shitty town we were temporarily squatting in.

"Cole intercepted me when I was leaving." I didn't tell her about the video. Partly so she wasn't involved, but I also secretly got off on one-upping him"

"Hold the fuck up!" Cassie leaned forward and grabbed my ankle for emphasis. Her blue eyes were wide with shock. "You waited until now to tell me that you snuck off with Cole for the night?"

"Ah, no." My lip curled of its own accord at the thought. "It wasn't like that. But…"

"But what? Woman, you're driving me crazy. Spill it."

"He dragged me into this small room in the field house. I think the maintenance crew uses that area because there were lockers."

"Yeah, those aren't the details I'm after." Cassie shook my leg.

I laughed. "I figured." Pushing out a breath, I got ready to tell her everything. "He kissed me, and it was… the most erotic thing I've ever experienced. I mean, it wasn't sweet or gentle. It was like you said, back-against-the-wall"—I grinned, knowing she would appreciate this part—"mouth fucking."

"Holy shit." Cassie laughed, just like I knew she would. "Then what happened?"

I shrugged, slightly uncomfortable. "I shoved him away and bolted."

Her mouth fell open, and I rolled my eyes at her dramatics, even though I felt them so hard too. I'd started to explain why when my door opened and terror filled me. *Please don't let it be Cole.* If he'd heard anything I'd said, I would die.

When a blond head came into sight, I sagged against the headboard, feeling weak from circumventing a potential disaster. "What are you doing here, Mom?"

"What do you mean?" She walked over to the bed and climbed on like we would all have some girl talk. "I live here too. Hi, I'm Raelyn, Riley's mom."

She smiled at Cassie, who looked at me to judge my reaction, which was sheer annoyance. She took the hint. "I'm Cassie. It's nice to meet you. Hey, Riley, I've got to go, but call me later, okay?"

I gave her a slow nod, my eyes telegraphing "coward" as she left. I didn't mean it, though. The last thing I needed was my new friend to witness what would happen next. Neither of us said a word until we heard the front door close.

"Why are you here?" Icicles hung from my words.

Mom stood up and started pacing. "Look, I get it that you're mad. You have every right to be. I've kept you in the dark, and it isn't even bad."

"So this *is* a con?" A spark of hope filled me. *Please say yes and that it's done so we can get the hell out of here.* That last part didn't feel completely right. For the first time, I had a friend. Like a real one. And even though Cole and his Elite group of assholes and the bitch crew were a nightmare, I could handle them. Then there was that kiss… and I hated to say it, but a part of me wanted to see where it led.

"No, it's not a con. I like Lucas. Well, more than that, actually."

"Since when? This is the first time I'm hearing about him."

"We have history. There wasn't much to tell, so I never thought much about it. Remember when we were in New York?"

"Yeah." I didn't like where this was going.

"It was his law firm I worked for, and we met, even had drinks a time or two."

"You slept with him?"

Red infused her cheeks. She stopped pacing and sat across from me on the bed. "Yeah, I did. Just once, but it was… different. Something I held onto. It felt real. And that's not something I was used to. Of course, it freaked me out, and then we left for that con in Connecticut."

"How did you reconnect?" I didn't blame her for sleeping with a guy, and she tended to overshare with me. I was cool with it because our relationship was unique. She was still a fierce protector, of course.

She did run away from whoever my father was and raised me on her own, which was proof enough. There had been other situations, too, but it wasn't the time for a trip down memory lane. "Mom." She still hadn't answered me about how they'd reconnected.

"He found me." She whispered.

"What?" I sat up straight. He could only mean one person. "Dad found you?"

"Oh, God." Her eyes widened in horror. "No. I'm so sorry. I didn't mean to freak you out. Not Dad, Lucas. I don't know how it happened. Well, I do, but I'm still a little in shock about it. But"—she waved away her own rambling—"here's the thing. He doesn't just want us to move in with him. He also asked me to marry him."

I just sat there. *Did I hear her right?* "Marriage?"

She nodded.

"And he wants both of us to move in, not just you?"

"Yeah. Aren't you excited?" Her smile was small and contained, but I could see the joy barely hidden behind it.

I didn't trust myself to answer with more than one word. "Sure, but this isn't real. It never is." Tears misted her eyes, and I hated myself.

"I'm trying, Riles." She grabbed my hand in hers, pleading with me through her eyes. "For the first time since I was a pregnant teenager, I'm being myself. This is my chance. Our chance. He makes me feel safe."

That was what got me. I rubbed my temples. Neither of us was safe, and it made no sense that this guy made her feel different. She was making herself vulnerable to him. My heart kicked into a frantic pace. We never let anyone in for a damn good reason. A pang of guilt pierced me—I'd broken the ironclad pact too. I'd let Cassie in. "And when things go bad? If one of our marks catches up with us, if Lucas learns who we really are, what then?"

"He'll protect us."

I studied her closely. I'd never seen her so hopeful before. We were always hustling then running. She'd done everything to keep food on our table and a roof over our heads. Maybe I could give her this for once, at least while it lasted. Even though I thought better of it, I nodded.

"Yeah?" She laughed, and it was a carefree sound that I wasn't sure I'd ever heard before.

"Yeah." But all I could think about by agreeing was that I would be living with Cole.

Monday was everything it was supposed to be but much more terrible. What I wouldn't have given for unlimited coffee delivered straight to my system through an IV. I barely saw Cass except for lunch, which I was eternally grateful for. The rest of the day had been filled with annoying gnats hurling stupid things to try to cut me down.

The bell rang to signal the end of the class, and I made a dash for the bathroom that was close by while there was time. It was empty when I went in, fortunately. I did what I needed to then washed my hands.

The bathroom's paper towel dispenser creaked as I pulled several out to dry my hands before the last class of the day. It had been a long day. Piper had cornered me at the end of first period to call me a slut; Jessica rounded out third hour; Brooke just rolled her eyes when we passed in the hallway; and Teagan had tried to trip me in gym. Their antics were more annoying than anything, and I was tired, my patience close to snapping, from the emotional turmoil of moving into Cole's house.

I crumpled the paper towels then tossed them in the garbage as the door swung open and Piper stormed in. *Wonderful.* "What is it now?" I wanted something more than these stupid verbal games.

Her lips were pressed together so hard that the color had leached from them. I smirked, and she rushed me. Blue eyes blazing, she pointed at me within an inch of touching. "You need to stay away from Cole, or bad things will start happening to you."

"So you've said, yet he keeps coming back to me." Not my best lines, but whatever. And I ignored the "bad things" comment because I wasn't worried. After Cass filled me in on what they'd done to a girl who'd tried to get with Shane—they'd filled her shampoo with Nair—I'd made it a point not to shower after gym.

"It doesn't matter because you don't mean anything to him. You're just a little slut. A plaything that he'll tire of then come back to me. He always does." Something that looked suspiciously like hurt flared in her eyes. "I'm the one he loves."

I huffed. Couldn't help it. "Honey, that guy doesn't love anyone but himself. You need to get that through your head and move on. No guy is worth this type of crazy."

I saw the slap coming before it happened and grabbed her wrist with a tight grip. Then I shoved hard. She stumbled back a few steps before regaining her footing. Her hand found the door, and she yanked it open, delivering a final parting word before leaving. "You're going to regret that."

I hadn't expected anything less.

Piper and her little brigade didn't worry me. Cole did.

CHAPTER EIGHTEEN

COLE

I slammed my locker shut with force, and Phoenix raised an eyebrow. The girl whose locker was next to mine scurried away. People looked. I didn't care.

Riley was late this morning. I didn't want to unpack why it bothered me, but my cousin had other ideas.

"She's under your skin, cuz."

"I have a way to get her out."

"You're going to sleep with her? Think that's wise, since she's moving in tonight?"

I grinned, and by the look on his face, it was as dark in appearance as it felt on the inside. Weird that it was happening on a Monday night rather than over the weekend. "She'll be within easy reach. Besides, I'm not sure she knows where she's living yet."

Phoenix shook his head as he pushed off the locker and fell into step beside me on our way to class. "I hope you know what you're doing."

A ripple of annoyance slithered through me. "Just stick to the plan. Freeze her out. Let the girls do whatever they want."

Phoenix paused before heading into his class, wariness settling over his features. "Those girls are rabid."

I refrained from commenting. Some part of my plan didn't sit right with me. Besides, I didn't need to expand further on what I wanted to be done to her. After meeting her mom and finding out who she was, my resolve was set in stone. I moved down a couple of classrooms until I found mine, the judgmental weight of my cousin's stare on my back. We were usually on the same page, and I didn't like what was happening. He should have understood despite the single-mom thing. If his sperm-donor father was in town with a new family, it would have been all-out war.

The following two hours crawled by. Finally, the last bell rang, and after grabbing my books, I filed into the hall with the rest of the class and would soon cross paths with Riley. But when I rounded the corner, it was to find her surrounded by Piper, Brooke, Jessica, Teagan, and Tracey. The last one was a surprise. She was usually glued to Shane's side, but if she wanted to join in, all the merrier.

I hung back, waiting to see what happened and how Riley reacted to the girls' bullying. Phoenix wasn't wrong. Those girls were vicious when an outsider tried to infiltrate the upper echelon. Piper or someone who reported to her must have seen us together at Saturday night's fight.

From my position against the lockers, I could hear Piper's venom. The contrast between them was interesting, and I ignored Piper's rant to take them in for a moment. Piper was the epitome of a Barbie wannabe, but so many parts of her that hadn't needed to be altered in the first place were fake. Fake boobs—and I would know—nose job, and who knew what else she would do to herself over the years. She was beautiful but in a rich, plastic sort of way. I never did understand why she'd had the surgeries. But that was the thing with so many of the academy kids. Money wasn't an issue. But parental and peer pressure was a bitch. Not only did you have to succeed by getting into the best Ivy League or D1 school, but you also had to look the part.

I tuned back into what Piper was lecturing—bullying—Riley about. The funny thing was, you would never have known anything was wrong by looking at her face. The things Piper said seemed to roll right off Riley, and I grudgingly recognized how much I liked that.

"You're nothing." Piper stepped closer in her space. "A nobody. Ugly. I bet even your parents don't want you." She snickered. "And none of the guys that matter here do either."

Piper was very wrong about one thing. Well, two, but the ridiculous one was that Riley was gorgeous, so much more than Piper or any of her minions were or could be. With her long, wavy chestnut hair, warm brown eyes, and model-esque bone structure, I'd had to threaten more than one guy to stay away from her. She was pure temptation with a body that promised hours of sin.

Jessica edged closer. "And your clothes." She wrinkled her pixie nose as if she smelled something foul. "They're obviously from a thrift store."

Brooke surveyed Riley from head to toe. "Face it, girl, you don't fit."

Piper sneered and leaned close, but I could still see part of Riley's amused face. "You're just like your whore mother." Her finger drilled into Riley's chest. "Cole is mine. Stop throwing yourself at him. You reek of desperation."

"Yeah." Riley grinned, brushing Piper's finger away. A gleam entered her eyes, and I wondered how far she would let things go before she snapped. "So original. I'm shaking in my boots."

I straightened to intervene before things went too far. I wasn't sure why. Something about anyone but me harassing Riley didn't sit well. But I hesitated when it seemed that Tracey had something to say. Her cheeks were bright red, and her eyes sparkled with malice. "Stay away from Damon. He's mine."

I snorted. I'd always known Tracey had a darker side. Too bad Shane was so blinded by her readily accessible pussy to see it.

Riley's eyes widened at that one, and a deep, throaty laugh spilled from her full lips. I had to reach down and adjust myself. Damn it. I couldn't be around her without getting hard.

"You have nothing to worry about with Demon"—her grin turned wicked—"unless I decide I want him for myself. Then all bets are off, little hanger-on."

She'd tensed to launch herself at Riley, and for some odd reason, I didn't want her hurt. "Tracey." Probably because I didn't want to look at scratches when I fucked her. That had to have been why. "Damon's looking for you."

She visibly shuddered with the effort it took to shove her rage down and paste the fake-adoration mask back on. "Hey, Cole. Thanks!" She pivoted and hurried toward the athletic locker room, where my brother was suiting up for practice.

That was where I was supposed to be. Piper wrapped her claws around my arm and pressed the side of her breast against my bicep before purring my name. Irritation raced through me, and I shook her off, but not before catching the unbecoming shade of red that flooded her face. The girls stepped back as I grabbed Riley's arm and pulled her from their reach. I had a few things to say to her without an audience who could use the information against her. Tormenting her was for me alone.

When we were far enough away from the cheer squad and their glares, I pushed her back against a wall of lockers and caged her between my arms, which only caused vivid recollections of Saturday night to flood my mind.

She quirked her brow. "Is this a repeat of the other night when you manhandled me?"

"No, little stepsister."

Her upper lip curled in repulsion. "You're disgusting."

"And you're too easy."

She slapped her hands on my chest and shoved me, but I didn't move an inch. Instead, I took my time, visually caressing every inch of her.

"If you're done toying with me, I'm leaving."

I dropped one of my arms, giving her a way to escape. "I'm done. Until tonight. Maybe we'll have another... chat when you're in your new bedroom."

She glared then hurried toward the exit to the parking lot. Guess she knew about the move. I wonder if she and her mom had planned it. I trailed her movements until she was out of sight before breaking into a jog toward the locker room to change for practice.

I was going to have to try harder to break her.

CHAPTER NINETEEN

RILEY

My head thudded against the steering wheel. *Argghh!* Cole made me so mad. *Stepsister? What kind of comment was that? Not likely.*

I growled again, punching the horn in a loud blast of noise. Mom needed to snap out of it and face facts.

We weren't normal.

Lucas wouldn't keep her safe.

Playing at a fairytale life wasn't in our cards.

I was so preoccupied with how conflicted I felt that I drove home on autopilot. With my head up and my hand on the door, I blinked my surroundings back into focus. A moving truck? I rubbed my eyes, hoping I was wrong.

Nope. There it was, a large white truck with black lettering on the side parked in front of our rental. Men went in and out, carrying boxes—the few belongings we had and that didn't warrant such a large truck.

I poured myself onto the driveway then stepped around the movers and rushed inside, my mind repeating one track: *this had better mean we're leaving this craptastic town and not what the dread lodged in my throat indicates.* I hurried through the living room and glanced in the kitchen but ultimately found her in my bedroom, taking my clothes from the dresser and putting them into my ratty old suitcase.

My backpack slid from my fingertips to land at my feet with a *thump*. "What are you doing? And please tell me that it isn't what I think it is. It better mean we're getting out of this nightmare town."

She scrunched her nose and gave me the look that meant I wasn't catching onto her plan quickly enough—which wasn't often. We thought alike, but sometimes, I was distracted, usually by teenage bullshit. She couldn't have known what moving so much did to me.

A wave of guilt followed on the heels of that thought. Of course she did. She stayed five steps ahead of anyone after us, mainly my dad—it was what drove her, and I knew firsthand that it wasn't easy because he'd found her once. We'd barely escaped with our lives, at least hers. He'd never found me. She'd made sure of it. Uncle Ronan had gotten word somehow and saved us.

A lock of dyed blond hair was tucked behind her ear, and she wore her favorite pair of faded form-fitting jeans and an old New York Jets T-shirt. "Nope, we're not leaving." Her features shuddered, and wariness replaced the openness I was used to seeing when it was just the two of us. "I told you we were moving into Lucas's home."

"Why so soon?" My body was numb. I would live under the same roof as Cole, *who hates me*. His threat replayed loudly in my head: *Maybe we'll have another... chat when you're in your new bedroom.* He'd had raw lust fueled by hate written all over his face. I spared a glance at Mom and the determination stamped on her face. There would be no talking her out of it.

Oh, Mom. What have you done? "Why did we move in here if you planned to move in with him in the first place?" My feet had grown roots. If only hers would too.

She paused in transferring a stack of shirts from the middle drawer to the suitcase, holding them suspended in her hands. "I had to ensure everything was in place and that Lucas meant what he'd said."

"And what was that, exactly?"

She resumed packing, breaking eye contact. "He loves me and is committed to this relationship no matter what I bring to the equation."

I stumbled back a step. "You mean me?"

Wide brown eyes met mine, and she reached out to me, but her hand never grasped mine because I tore myself free from the spot I was rooted to. My back hit the wall.

"No, Riley, that wasn't what I meant."

"Save it, Mom." Part of me knew I was being irrational, but I didn't care. I felt pushed into a corner, and I had to throw one last dig before I stormed over to the suitcase and grabbed a bathing suit. "Cole's an asshole who's been determined to make my life hell since the first day of school. But whatever, I'll figure it out, since we'll share a living space."

I didn't let her get a word in before I fled my room and the house. I suspected my suitcase was the last thing to pack, since the movers loitered around the truck. I tossed my backpack and bathing suit into the car. As I pulled out, I saw our sad boxes barely taking up a minute fraction of the truck. We kept things light and minimal because we moved frequently and often in the middle of the night. Our possessions had to be manageable and fit into two cars.

Mom wasn't naïve, but I was afraid she was only seeing what she wanted after so many years of struggling. And I got it. She deserved to be happy and, for once, have someone love her but not want to consume her soul. But I didn't think Lucas was the one who could keep her safe. I didn't know if such a man existed.

I floored it down the street. I could go to the high school's pool, but the last thing I wanted was to run into Cole again. The need to dive was almost crushing, and I knew I couldn't deny the part of myself that longed for the freedom it gave me. After pulling over to the side of the road, I grabbed my phone and texted Cassie: *Hey, busy?*

If you call watching cartoons with my little sister and doing home-work busy. What's up?

Know anywhere I can dive? Not school.

As a matter of fact—yes! I'll text you the address. It's a drive but worth it. Meet you there in twenty or so.

Thanks.

The address came through, and I typed it into my maps app. She wasn't kidding. It wasn't close. I settled into the leather seat, cranked the radio, then pulled onto the street, following the directions my phone read to me.

When I turned into the state park, my eyes were bugging out of my head. *Why didn't I know about this place already?* I spotted several tall cliffs and a sparkling cove upon pulling into the lot.

I hurried out of the car, slammed and locked the door, then went to the edge of the cove, where I dropped my bag. The water rippled—it looked deep enough to cliff dive from and like the perfect place to practice. There were several spots on the cliff soaring overhead where I could jump, but I had my eye on one about fifty feet up. There was a discreet restroom tucked into one area of the clearing, and I changed into my one-piece suit.

Since Cassie wasn't here and I didn't know if I could wait for her, I jumped into the water and swam around underneath, checking out the area to scope out hidden dangers I couldn't see from overhead. The water was warmer than the ocean and felt like bliss, which I desperately needed after the trainwreck earlier. And it wasn't over. I had to take full advantage, since this would keep my sanity intact for what I would face tonight in enemy territory.

I broke the surface. The area beneath was mapped in my mind, so I could dive safely. After pulling myself onto the rocky shore, I hurried up the path to the part of the cliff I'd been eyeballing, approximately fifty feet up and in the right position for a dive. Toes at the edge of the worn rock, I visualized my body turning and twisting before piercing the water with barely a ripple. The anticipation built, those tiny butterflies taking flight as my body tensed, knees bent. Harnessing the energy and setting the image to manifest, I pushed off the ledge.

To add speed, I tucked and flipped twice before opening into a layout, all tight lines and precise movements until breaking the surface with barely a splash. The water welcomed me, enveloping and catching my fall. Arching to change direction, I kicked to the surface, exhilarated and feeling lighter after only a single dive. I couldn't wait to get up there and do it again.

Cassie pulled up and got out of her car as I climbed out. "Hey, not cool. You shouldn't be cliff jumping without me here."

"You're here now." My smile stretched wide. "Are you jumping too?" She shrugged. Already in her bathing suit, she dropped a towel and her bag not far from where I stood.

"I'll jump but from that spot."

She pointed at the lowest outcropping to the right of where I'd been. "Let's go." As we climbed, I paused when she went to the lowest spot. "I'm going higher, but I'll wait until you jump."

"Okay, crazy." Cass winked before going to the edge. She took a few deep breaths then jumped, screaming the entire way down.

I looked over to see her land with a big splash. When she surfaced, I couldn't keep the laughter in. "You all right?"

"If by 'all right,' you mean, 'did I see my entire life flash before my eyes,' then yes."

I shook my head before pivoting to return to the trail and the same ledge as before. I could barely contain my excitement. It was gorgeous here, and the freedom to try things I'd never done at a pool's high dive was like a shot of pure adrenaline. There were combinations I'd watched repeatedly from the Olympics, and I wanted to do them too. No boards, even the academy's, were high enough. But here… I could do anything I wanted, even make my own.

I made sure she'd cleared the cove before I pictured the combination of flips I wanted to do. The familiar anticipation built, and then I jumped, soaring through the air before maneuvering my body to produce the twists and turns I'd visualized.

Making my body into an arrow from fingers to toes, I hit the water with precision. Stress evaporated. I felt invigorated, free, and happy.

It was what I was meant to do with my life. I couldn't deny it any longer.

Arching, I kicked for the surface, leaving one dimension for another. My head broke the surface, and I inhaled warm air and struck out for the shore.

Tiny rocks mixed with sand and dirt bit into the soles of my feet. It was quiet, and I jolted when Cass stepped in front of me, her eyes wide.

"You've been holding out on me. That was…"

I grinned. This was the first time someone other than my family had watched me dive like that. It felt so good that I wanted more.

Mom's words played in my head about staying here for the year.

Could I?

Hell yes! I was going to join the diving team at the academy.

CHAPTER TWENTY

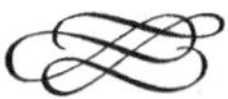

COLE

"Where's the rest of your stuff?" Somehow, Riley had managed to avoid me at school, but we were both home tonight. I'd found her room and positioned myself in her doorway, leaning against the edge of it and effectively blocking her in.

I'd come home late last night. We'd had football practice then sparring.

I could smell her lilac-and-honey scent tempting me to come closer. I didn't trust myself to step foot in her room—not yet.

In a slow pivot, she faced me with a handful of bathing suits clutched tightly in her hands. Visually, I traced her profile. Her long wavy hair cascaded down her back, rippling as she unpacked boxes and put her things away in the already furnished room. There were so few boxes. I couldn't believe it when I saw what the movers had brought in and stacked in the room. Raelyn's shit was, of course, in my dad's room. And one small box for the kitchen would probably go in the garage, since we didn't need whatever they had.

"This is it."

"For real? There has to be more stashed somewhere. You've

got what? A few weeks' worth of clothes at most?" And one picture. I zeroed in on that, pushing myself off the doorjamb and casually strolling to where I'd spotted it nestled in her suitcase, visible under the layer of clothes she'd removed. Through my haze of anger and annoyance, her lack of belongings bothered me, and I wanted to know if the rest of their stuff was elsewhere. Another family that my blinded-by-pussy dad hadn't found, maybe, or even a storage locker somewhere. "Do you move a lot?"

She ignored me until she figured out what I'd found. I picked up a plastic picture frame that housed a photo of her and her mom, arm in arm, with big goofy smiles on their faces. It had to have been fairly recent. I studied the mountains in the background, trying to place where it had been taken.

A small huff sounded beside me before she snatched the picture from my hand. "Get out."

I grinned, feeling the darkness inside me grow and stretch alongside her panicky exasperation. I'd struck a nerve somewhere, probably with the glimpse into what she cared about most clearly visible in the frame. Her mom. Wonder how she'd react or what she would do when I went after Raelyn. I wasn't above extortion.

Riley twisted my mind in too many ways, and the thought of her sleeping in one of the rooms in our house was enough for me to know I had to tire myself out so I would pass out as soon as my head hit the pillow. I'd accomplished that.

She slammed the lid to her suitcase, blocking me from checking out the facedown picture that I hadn't noticed before. It didn't matter, though. I would be back, and there was little she could do to stop me.

"We may have to live in the same house, but I don't have to put up with you." She sneered then shoved my chest.

"That's where you're wrong." I grabbed her wrist before she could move away and backed her against the wall. Frustration vibrated off her in waves. I had her right where I wanted and closed the distance between us so that our faces were barely an inch apart. "Sleep tight. I'll be right across the hallway if you need anything."

She flashed me a disgusted look.

Addicted to her scent, I leaned in, my face at the side of her neck before I knew what I was doing. I breathed her in. She shivered. It was enough of a win for the time being.

Releasing her, I left without a word or even a second look. Once in my room, I shut the door behind me so I could focus on the research I needed to do. I wanted to know why she and her mom moved around so much that her things could fit into a couple of boxes.

I looked up when a knock sounded on my door. Damon opened it, and I tossed a pen at him. "Come on in."

"Just did." He winked before falling onto my bed. "I was coming upstairs when I heard Dad's car in the driveway. Want to do a little recon?"

"Hell, yes." I closed my laptop, abandoning my research for the time being, and we took care not to make a sound as we went downstairs and followed the voices, stopping in the hallway just out of sight. We could see them enter the kitchen. Raelyn dropped her purse on the island, pausing in front of Dad when he tucked a few strands of her hair behind her ear.

"I liked your hair the way it was. You didn't have to dye it."

"Yeah, I did. I'm going to all these client functions with you. The odds are high that one of them knows him. Or a picture will be taken of us and that'll be it. This"—she grabbed a chunk of her hair—"isn't a perfect disguise, but it's helped in the past, and I can't take a chance with Riley. If he finds us…"

Determination hardened Dad's face into stone. "He won't."

"You know that's not realistic." Her eyes glistened. It was a nice touch. "I have to anticipate that he will so we can survive."

"I promised you that I would protect you both, and I mean to do that." He brushed a kiss across her mouth before embracing her.

She rested her head on his chest, her face turned toward where Damon and I were shielded by shadow in the hallway. I didn't miss the tears clinging to her lashes. "And what about your sons? He's not above using anyone to draw us out."

I blinked in the inky darkness of my room, confused at what had woken me. Fumbling on the nightstand for my phone, I pressed the button so the screen would light and I could read the time: one o'clock in the morning. My phone fell out of my hands to clatter back on the table, and I scrubbed my hands over my face when my stomach growled.

Somehow, with everything going on, I'd skipped dinner. There was no way I could go back to sleep so hungry, so I got up and went to the kitchen to make a sandwich. My hand curled around the cool banister, and I took care to skip the squeaky steps on the way down. A soft sound cut through the hum of the first floor, and I paused, listening. There it was again. The glide of a slider as it shut, and I knew that what had most likely woken me, aside from my stomach, was the creak in the stairs closest to my room.

It was a good thing I didn't have shoes on as I crept through the living room to peer carefully out onto the lanai. It took a while to scan the dark interior, but I didn't see anyone, which meant that whoever it was had gone out the sliders that led to the pool. I flipped the lock and inched the door open. When there was enough room for me to squeeze through, I did. Rather than risk any additional noise, I left it open. No light spilled out from the house, but I could hear voices coming from the outdoor seating area closest to the house.

The screened-in porch was the best place to spy on whoever was out there because of the overabundance of plants that filled it. With care, I maneuvered around the furniture to the heavy foliage closest to the voices. It had sounded like a woman's voice, and as I waited, I heard Raelyn's hushed words.

There was enough light for me to see her outline as she stood close to a man whose face I couldn't make out.

"I want you to meet him, but the timing still isn't right."

"I don't think we should wait much longer, not if what you told me about is in the works." I strained to hear his deep, much-harder-to-hear voice.

"I know. But... I need to get this worked out. Give me a little more time."

He hugged her, and I could just make out her whispered "I love you."

Shock held me immobile as she released him then let herself back inside. Coming to my senses, I did the same, softly closing the slider and flipping the lock just as I heard the alarm reactivate. I stayed where I was, annoyed with myself for not bringing my phone downstairs. If I had, I would have recorded them. There was nothing I could do about it, and I waited until I heard Raelyn move through the house and back up the stairs.

Sandwich forgotten, I returned to my room, doubting that I would be able to go back to sleep. I didn't have enough to go on to bring it to my dad. I would get to the bottom of whatever that had been. If there was one thing I was sure about, it was that Raelyn was hiding something.

I planned to discover what that was.

CHAPTER TWENTY-ONE

RILEY

My skin itched like hundreds of fiery red ants were crawling on me. The house was huge and not where I belonged.

I dug my heels into the wood floor and shoved the desk chair on an angle. With my back to the corner, I could see the door and window. Heavy clouds crowded the sky with the threat of rain. The air felt charged… or maybe it was just me.

My gaze skipped over the picturesque backyard, which contained both a pool and a hot tub. It was crazy to think that Cole and Damon lived like this. I knew they were entitled, but I'd found myself swept up in their world, and I didn't know what to make of it.

If only they had a high dive, I would have sold my soul, too, just like Mom had.

A familiar, soft knock sounded at my door. As she padded across the wood floor to my side, I tore my gaze from the pool, and my sight landed on Mom.

"Hey." She perched on the edge of my desk, looking more like herself than the Stepford version I'd glimpsed since we moved here.

"Hey, yourself." I couldn't keep the bitterness from my tone. I was still mad. What had happened to her and me against the world? I was still reeling from the one-eighty she'd done, all in the name of love, or so she'd said. I had trouble with the thought of her truly loving Cole's dad. It seemed odd.

She tugged on a strand of my hair before releasing it. "How are you adjusting to this house? Crazy, isn't it?"

"You call it a house. I call it a mansion."

"Yeah..." She did a visual sweep of my large bedroom. "Our entire apartment in New York could fit in here. I'm still not used to it."

"About that. You really think it's good to get used to this?"

Mom pursed her lips. "Riley, everything will be okay. I promise."

Thunder rumbled, followed by the soft patter of rain against the glass windowpane. The fine hairs on the back of my neck stood up, and I couldn't help the sense of dread that formed at her words. "We don't do that," I whispered, not bothering to explain. She knew what I meant about impossible promises.

She shook her head, her dyed blond hair shimmering around her shoulders. I preferred the golden shade she'd worn when we first got to this stupid town or her natural brunette. It was less Stepford. "I met Lucas in New York when you were a few months old. He was on winter break and about to start his last semester of college. When we saw each other for the first time in Central Park... something sparked between us. I don't even know how to explain it. I've never felt anything so powerful. He provided a respite from the crushing fear that I was screwing everything up. I was seventeen and so, so scared."

My mouth went dry, and I shifted, trying to find comfort where there was very little. "What happened?"

"There isn't much to tell. I had a whirlwind affair with him while he was in town. It didn't last more than a few weeks. Then someone who shouldn't have spotted me did, and I knew it was time to leave. I never said goodbye to him. Ronan got us out and to someplace safe until we could figure out where to go."

"Why didn't you ever tell me about him before?"

She shrugged. "And say what? I met someone after your father and fell in love with him but ditched him before anything could come of it? There was no point. Lucas and I couldn't have a future. I thought we wouldn't cross paths again. But we did. And the next time I ran into him was last year, and he had a wife, which you knew. Things went south fast, and I wasn't interested in getting mixed up in that. He didn't think the timing was right either. It wasn't until he found me again that we moved back here and I decided to give us the chance that he asked for."

I narrowed my eyes at her. "He's a cheater, then." At Mom's nod, a sick sensation swept over me. "What's to stop him from doing the same to you?"

Movement drew my focus to the door where Lucas stood. "Because she's the one for me. I would have done anything to be with her, but she disappeared—twice—and I gave up hope."

Mom winked then got off my bed. She could read me well enough to know I was thoroughly creeped out. "We're heading to the city for a few days." She worried her lower lip, looking unsure. "Will you be all right here, Riles?"

"Cole and Damon will be here," Lucas said.

Unhelpful. I could tell that was what concerned her too. She opened her mouth to say something, probably to announce that she'd changed her mind about leaving me, but I wasn't going to let Lucas see any weakness. Because when things went to hell, and they would, I didn't want him to have any ammunition to use.

"Yep. I'll be fine." My gaze never strayed from Lucas's blue eyes. I didn't trust him after my interactions with his spawn.

They left with his arm around her waist, and I had an irra-tional urge to get up and slam the door. I pulled out my homework and forced myself to finish it, even though I wanted to jump in my car and head to the cove. It was rainy, though, and I doubted Cass would go with me.

Forty-five minutes later, I could no longer ignore how loudly my stomach was growling. I left the sanctuary that my room had become in a house I was unsure of and ventured to the kitchen. With the enormous island in sight, I pictured everything I would make. We'd never had a kitchen like this. It was beautiful and fully stocked. But when I got closer, I noticed their housekeeper, Louisa, at the stove.

"Hi." *Awkward.* I had no idea what to do. We'd never had anyone cook or clean for us before. It was weird.

She turned from the stove and smiled. Her kind eyes lit up, and she set the spoon down before going to the fridge. "Hello, Riley. Mr. Savage told me you would be staying with us. Sit. Would you like a sandwich or something else?"

"A sandwich is fine."

She waved to the island before opening the fridge and taking out bread, a tomato, lettuce, and sandwich meat. "Mayo?"

"Ah, no thanks." I eased onto one of the stools, my back stiff. I didn't know what to do with my hands, so I threaded my fingers together and rested them on my lap. She put the sandwich together on a plate, got an apple and cut it up, too, then put it in front of me. "Thank you. I hope you don't mind if I take it to my room?" I didn't know what the rules were and felt strange about her making me a sandwich in the first place.

"Of course not."

I repeated my thanks for the third time then hurried from the kitchen and to the stairs. I had my head down as I raced up, not paying attention. There must have been a sound. I couldn't remember why I looked up, but I did, and good thing, too, because Cole was leaning against the wall not far from the landing. *Great.* Not what I needed after the whole bizarre day.

I raised my chin and tried to walk by him.

He put his arm out, blocking me.

"What do you want?"

He said nothing, just took half my sandwich and scarfed it down in three bites. When I snapped out of watching how his throat moved when he swallowed, I tucked my plate closer to my body. The jerk could have gotten his own food. There was also no way I was sharing the rest or going back to get more—it was too uncomfortable. I stepped to the side. He didn't try to stop me. My pace quickened as I neared my room, and I hoped he wasn't following me, but the hairs on the back of my neck said otherwise. My fingers closed on the edge of my door, and I whipped it behind me to slam it shut. No sound came.

Of course he was in my room.

"Why are you here?' I set the plate on my desk harder than I'd meant to.

"Met your mom." He grabbed a slice of apple.

I shrugged, glaring at each bite he took. "You met her before when you all went to lunch. Hardly see how that's news."

"She was cagey about where you came from." He strolled around my room, stopping at the small stack of books I had, picking one up and looking at the title before replacing it. "Since you're living in my house, there are things I need to know."

I snorted. "I'm sure your father would've found anything pertinent. You don't matter, since this is ultimately your father's house. It's his decision who lives here, not yours." I bit into the apple to keep from smiling. I'd hit a nerve, evident by the color staining his cheeks.

"Don't think you and your gold-digger mom are safe here." He closed the distance between us and leaned over me, hooking a finger under my chin and holding me in place. "One of you'll break, and then I'll learn everything about your past, your family, and how to take you down."

His hand fell away, and I hated how I craved his touch, how

a fire burned inside me at something so simple. Without a word, he pushed off my desk and left. A tremor ran through me in the wake of his threat. I couldn't let him find out anything about our past, and that asshole was not going after my mom. I still had an ace up my sleeve with the career-ending video.

If he wanted a war, I would give him one.

CHAPTER TWENTY-TWO

COLE

Riley drove me crazy.

I couldn't stop thinking about her. The softness of her skin. The way her breath hitched at the first touch of my hand. How her pupils dilated. The sheer fieriness of her personality.

I needed to do something about her.

Phoenix and I sat in the basement, watching the fight on TV. It was only the two of us in the house, other than Riley, who'd holed up in her room. She'd gone out, and judging by the faint scent of chlorine when she'd returned, I guessed she'd snuck into the school to dive. Irritation that she'd moved into my territory—both home and school.

"This fight sucks." I grabbed our empty beer bottles and stood to get more when I realized what I needed to do. "My dad will be out of town all weekend. Let's have a party." I glanced at Phoenix. "Text everyone." Usually, I would schedule a cleaning service for the next day. But not this time.

Damon and I might transfer cash from our fights into Phoenix and Shane's accounts for school, but we always set aside enough for situations in which we needed to hire a stellar cleaning service after a bash. I was saving the money for another time. I welcomed the mess.

We also had our trusts, but Dad had access until we turned twenty-one and would see if we made any withdrawals. Money wasn't an issue for us. Our cousins needed it for college, but we had some immediate priorities, at least until our dad agreed to release our trust funds when we went to college. That was one thing we'd negotiated with him when he'd hijacked control after Mom died. She'd set them up with the stipulation that we would have access once we graduated high school. Everything changed in so many ways when she died.

It was another reason why Riley and her mom needed to pay. And tonight, I would make it clear that Riley didn't belong here.

An hour later, while Phoenix and I were setting up a station with Solo cups and a keg, Damon strolled in with Jessica trailing behind, excitement lighting up her face as she texted on her phone.

"Let me guess, Dad's in the city with his new whore?" My brother laughed, and I socked him in the arm.

"Not now." My glare said it all—*shut up about our problems*—and he grabbed Jessica's hand and pulled her to the keg to get her a drink. He knew better than to air our shit in front of anyone. Of the two of us, I hated our dad more than Damon did, but what had broken our mom had pushed him over the edge too.

Within five minutes, fifty people showed up, and another hundred after that. Music pumped through the house, and the beer was flowing. The party was in full swing as I downed another beer, my fifth, counting the minutes until Riley made her presence known.

Piper hung off my arm, and I let her. I needed this plan to work, despite whatever would happen at school in the aftermath.

Tracey had her hooks in Shane, planning to ride his coattails, and Piper had a similar idea. She was smart and didn't need the career I planned to have to coast through life, but she was in love with me—an emotion I did not return. Not only that, but I warned her when we hooked up randomly that it didn't mean we were dating, even though I was exclusive with her for the better part of last year.

It was her choice, and she always said yes. She thought she could wear me down and coerce me into something more permanent. I was too fucked up for a relationship. I don't know why she couldn't see it.

Phoenix passed me a shot. Piper frowned, and his grin stretched wider. "Tracey's got the ones for you and Jessica." He waved behind him, managing to keep the liquor in the small glass. "They're over there somewhere."

"You're such an asshole," Piper hissed.

We clinked glasses while she stormed off. "What's the plan here?" He didn't miss anything. Phoenix and I had a lot in common. He thought a few steps ahead, too—he had to as the quarterback.

"I'm waiting for Riley to get pissed off enough that she comes downstairs."

His brows climbed his forehead. "I didn't realize she was here. When did that happen?"

"She and her mom moved in yesterday."

"And you plan to have them moving out just as quickly?" Phoenix glanced toward the stairs then chuckled. He slapped me on the back. "Think you're about to get your chance to make something happen."

My cousin took a step back, his arm automatically going around the waist of a girl he'd been eyeing while talking to me. I felt Riley's presence with heightened awareness, almost like an electrical current, before I saw her. Piper's eyes went wide before they turned stormy, tossing her cup at one of the other girls before pushing through them to stake her claim by my side. I turned just as Riley made her way down the stairs. My muscles tensed with the urge to go to her, but I waited. She had to come to me.

I allowed myself one glance, making sure she spotted me. When she did, I turned away but got my phone ready, ticking down the seconds in my head. Her lilac-and-honey scent with a hint of chlorine wrapped around me, and her fingers grazed my bicep before she dug them in to get my attention. What she didn't know was that she'd had it all along.

My arm snaked around her waist, and I pulled her close before snapping a few selfies of us with the party in the background. I had seconds before Piper would reach us and needed to take full advantage.

I skimmed Riley from head to toe. She was in tiny sleep shorts with graphics of to-go coffee cups and a tight T-shirt. Her arms were crossed over her breasts, trying to hide herself, but it was her hooded eyes and just-fucked hair that stole my breath. Damn, she was hot. She looked sleepy, which would translate to drunk in the pictures I'd taken.

A pang of longing hit me unexpectedly. *If only things were different.* But they weren't, and I hardened myself to the seductress I planned to destroy.

She took in the out-of-control party and then narrowed her heated eyes on mine. "Want to stop the wide-scale destruction?"

I shrugged. "It's my father's house. Doesn't matter."

"You're spoiled." She spat the words just as Piper shoved her way through the last group of people separating us.

"What's that whore doing here?" Piper stood in front of Riley and me with her arms crossed over her angrily heaving chest.

I grinned, my hand locking around Riley's as she tried to escape upstairs. "Haven't you heard, Pipes? Riley's mom's screwing my dad. She lives here now." That dropped like a bomb, rippling through the crowd.

"You're an asshole." Riley yanked her hand away then shoved through throngs of partygoers and to the stairs.

Anger raced through me, and I lunged after her. People moved out of my way. She had no idea what my life was like or what my brother and I had been through.

Her furious stride gave her a head start, but she wasn't fast enough, and I cleared the landing and slapped my palm against her bedroom door mid-slam. I caught it and slammed it closed behind us, turning the lock before cornering her at the bed. "Do not walk away from me." Fury mixed with lust sizzled around me. She drove me crazy, and I hated how fucking soft she looked and how amazing she smelled.

Her breath came in short little pants, fire crackling from her eyes, and her nipples hardened. I needed a taste. Just one. Leaning into her, I buried my hand in the back of her hair, fisting it so she couldn't move as I whispered, "You have no right to judge me."

"Don't think—"

I slammed my mouth over hers, stopping her words. She was pissing me off. And I needed to taste her. The feel of her plump lips beneath mine… decadent. I slipped past her lips when she gasped, tangling my tongue with hers.

She melted. Her body pressed against mine, heating every inch where she touched, and I hardened, desperate for more.

I tugged her hair, angling her head for better access. Goddammit, she tasted and felt so fucking good. The effect she had on me was like nothing I'd experienced before. I knew I needed to stop, but I couldn't.

CHAPTER TWENTY-THREE

RILEY

Cole held me in place with a firm grip on my hair, his mouth devouring mine. Heat pooled low in my belly, and I moaned into the kiss, clinging to his shoulders as my heart raced. All my resistance and hatred fled at the first touch of his lips. Flames licked my skin, nerve endings on fire as he broke the kiss, trailing more along my jaw and then my neck. My head fell back to give him greater access.

In the back of my mind, I knew it was wrong. I hated him. But for the life of me, I couldn't bring myself to stop. I craved his touch. Heat pooled low in my belly, and my thighs squeezed together against the throbbing ache. I'd never felt like that with anyone before, and it took me entirely by surprise and threw me off my game.

The steady beat of bass and drums from the overly loud music one floor below, mixed with what must have been our entire school, faded. There was only him.

I should have expected to be so off-balance, even as my hands crawled over his back, feeling the muscles bulge and flex. He'd pressed his body against mine before, when I looked like someone else. He hadn't figured that out yet. But I knew, and the knowledge gave me a sliver of power.

His teeth scraped against my lower lip before he nipped it. I squirmed against him, on sensory overload. When his fingers slipped beneath my shirt, trailed over my stomach, then cupped my breast, I moaned. Nothing mattered but what he was doing. I tugged at his shirt, needing to feel his skin.

With deft fingers, he removed both my shirt and his before lowering me to the white duvet that covered my queen-sized bed. Cool air danced over my skin, and I shivered. I lay there, vulnerable and exposed, while his lust-filled gaze crawled over me in a visual caress. The tangible desire between us was the only thing that kept me from leaping off the bed and covering myself.

I took in his chiseled chest. I knew he was ripped, since I'd seen him without a shirt, but not like that, not when I could feel him. My fingers twitched to touch him, to run over the bumps and ridges of his abs and the defined swell of his biceps, and clasp onto his strong, broad shoulders as he lowered himself over me. I welcomed his weight, the hard pressing of his thick length between my thighs, our clothes the only barrier from stopping what I wanted more than my next breath.

He rolled my nipple between the pads of his fingers. I shifted closer, and he moved onto his side, only partially covering me. We had better access to explore one another that way, and I was taking full advantage as his lips descended on my breast, taking my nipple into his mouth and sucking. He released it with a pop when my hand grazed the front of his jeans. Intent on touching more of him, I popped the button then slid the zipper down. My heart was pounding furiously. I didn't know what I was doing. I hadn't ever done this before. But I was going on instinct and raw need. I just hoped he couldn't tell how inexperienced I was.

My other hand sank into his short, soft hair. He deepened the kiss, and I swore I saw stars. If kissing was a sport, he was an

Olympic athlete, playing my body like a fine-tuned instrument. I squirmed against his hand as he trailed it low then under the waistband of my sleep shorts. Stopping at the apex of my thighs, he teased me by brushing his thumb over my panties. I squirmed, desperate for more. He changed direction, tracing the edge of my panties in a feather-light touch that tormented me further. Two could play at that game. I narrowed my eyes, catching the silver glow of moonlight that spilled across his sinful features.

My hand curled around his hardness, silk stretched over steel, and I squeezed him. Every inch of him froze. His muscles seemed to swell and tighten, and I suddenly found myself drowning in the intensity of his attention. It was powerful and intimidating. But I refused to back down and gave him a slow stroke. He shuddered over me before tearing the cotton of my panties away. Then he gave me what I wanted, the glide of his finger between my lips, spreading the silky heat of desire that pooled over my clit. I gasped, shuddering as he dipped a single finger inside me.

My hand tightened as I remembered what I was doing. My thumb caressed the smooth head, spreading the pearly bead that had gathered at the tip, coating the palm of my hand before sliding up and down, setting a rhythm that had him groaning and quickening the pace of his finger inside me. Then there were two, stretching and adding pressure.

My body tightened around him like a vise. He knew what I needed and exactly how to do it. When his fingers curled deep inside me, applying pressure, I arched into him. Another pump, and he moaned, and then his lips were at the base of my neck, where my shoulder met it, and my pulse beat frantically. He sucked and teased the sensitive spot. I kept my hand moving, feeling him grow harder and longer. I wasn't going to last, and I wanted him to fall with me.

With a swirl of his thumb over my clit, a slight pressure, I tumbled over the edge, arching against him. His mouth covered mine, swallowing my scream in a drugging kiss. He shuddered, pumping into my hand twice more, then came with me.

We didn't move, our rapid breathing slowly regulating. My body pulsed around his fingers, still inside me, and I was in awe. I'd never felt a fraction of what he'd made me feel. I'd completely lost control, and that wasn't normal. Not only that, but deep inside, I feared he'd imprinted himself in my DNA. I didn't know if I would ever be the same again.

I let my eyes drift shut, coming to terms with what just happened. The enormousness of the situation and what could follow next. Because I didn't know, and that terrified me. I didn't like it one bit. I wasn't used to being so out of control.

He slowly pulled his fingers out and disentangled my hand from his cock. He grabbed his shirt and cleaned himself up before doing the same to my hand. I was limp, my limbs weighted and heavy. I didn't want to move. I didn't want him to move, either, and a wave of vulnerability swept over me strongly enough to raise my awareness of my situation. He hadn't said a word, and I watched him warily.

When our eyes met, I shivered at the coldness and the complete lack of emotion reflected in his.

Then he walked out, leaving the door open. I leaped out of bed on his heels. At the open door, I put all my weight behind it and slammed it shut, letting out a scream of frustration. That fucker. I would get him back for that. I flipped the lock, fighting tears, and grabbed my phone, sending him the video before I second-guessed myself then flopped face-first onto my bed.

I'm such an idiot.

CHAPTER TWENTY-FOUR

COLE

The quiet buzz from my phone's alarm vied for supremacy over the loud rumble of thunder outside. *It's time.* Already awake, I hadn't needed either sound and slipped into the hallway, alert and ready. It was the perfect night to search Riley's room.

My fingers curled around her doorknob only to find it locked. A silent laugh escaped. I came prepared for that and pulled the paper clip from my pocket. With a tug on one end of the thin metal, I straightened enough to slip into the small hole in the knob and popped the lock.

The house was silent. No one was awake. Three in the morning was the perfect time to break into her room and delete the video she'd taken of the illegal fight. I had to wipe every trace of it—it could ruin my brother and cousins along with me, once an investigation was underway. I would not let that happen.

It infuriated me that she'd threatened their futures, whether knowingly or not.

Dad would pay off any threats. I suspected Damon and I would be fine. But our cousins would not, and I couldn't let her destroy their lives before they even entered Thane and the football field that would be the next stepping stone in their career. If the video went live, there would be a battle ahead for them even to attend the university, let alone play football. Money, always an issue for them, would seem impossible, especially since their shithead sperm donor refused to help or even acknowledge them.

I slipped inside the dark bedroom, closing the door behind me with a tiny click. I held still for several seconds and waited to ensure that she remained asleep. When no sound came, I pressed the side button on my phone for a little light.

She lay on her side, away from the window. Her hair fanned across the pillow, and the sheet was pulled back to reveal one long, slender leg with skin so soft I could lose myself in her for days. She was stunningly gorgeous, and I didn't think she knew or cared. One look was all it took, and she held me in the palms of her hands. She just didn't know it, and I needed to keep it that way.

I hated that I wanted her.

Tearing my eyes from her, I went to where her phone lay on the nightstand beside the bed. I swiped the screen but found it locked, of course. Good thing she was nearby. Holding the camera in front of her face, I unlocked it quickly and moved away. Once in the videos, I located the one she'd sent me and deleted it from there and her trash. I went through her texts to me and deleted the video there, too, and any other place it could be.

There were no locked folders. That left anyone else she could have texted or emailed with the incriminating recording. When I came across the thread between her and Cass, I took my time and read it all. There wasn't anything incriminating, but it told me enough. She confided in Cass. It was information I filed away in case I needed to use it.

I returned the phone to the nightstand and searched her

room for a USB drive. Rain pelted against the windowpanes, and lightning strobed, finding entrance through the gaps in the bottom of the blinds where she hadn't pulled them down.

There wasn't anything on her computer tucked away in her drawers or pockets. I'd checked. But I kept coming back to her phone. After palming it, I swiped the screen and looked at her contacts. There were four. That was it. I knew two of them because of the text stream: Raelyn and Cass. The third was mine. But the fourth was a mystery, and so was the lack of data, including any texts between her and the person she'd labeled just as R.

I replaced the phone again. It bothered me. Even if it had been a newer phone, there would've been a data transfer. No one had so little information on their phones, which brought me back to something being very off with her and Raelyn.

A loud crack of thunder boomed, and I froze as Riley turned onto her back in her sleep. I waited for her eyes to open. But they never did, and I relaxed. I needed to get out of there, but I couldn't resist moving closer. She had that effect on me. With a featherlight touch, I cupped her cheek. Her skin was like silk, and a deep sense of possessiveness exploded inside my chest. I snatched my hand back, disturbed by how little control I had over myself.

As silently as I'd entered her room, I exited, remembering to flip the lock on her doorknob so she would never know I was there. Back in my room, I changed clothes to work out, needing to burn off some excess energy.

With several hours before school, I headed to our home gym in the basement. I had to admit it: the war Riley and I had going on was the most fun I'd had in a long time. The ball was back in my court, and I couldn't wait to see her reaction when I laid that on her.

In desperate need of coffee, I went downstairs, fully dressed and ready for football practice. Sunlight streamed through the windows, mocking the start of a new day after a raging storm and nearly sleepless night, thanks to Riley's text with the video of my fight. I tried to catch a few hours after kicking everyone out of the house, but I couldn't get the way Riley felt, tasted, and sounded out of my mind.

She was hurt. I understood that. This girl… if I wasn't hell-bent on running her and her mom out of town, I would have loved for things to be different. Because with her, they already were.

Wading through a sea of Solo cups, my shoes sticking to the floor with each step, I rounded the island. Bread went into the toaster. And after popping a pod into the machine, I set a mug down and waited for it to brew, leaning against the counter and counting the seconds until both were ready.

The staff would be here soon, and I was glad that Louisa had the weekend and half of this week off for her daughter's wedding. Having her walk into this mess and feeling the need to clean didn't sit right with me.

Until Louisa returned, we would be on our own for meals. As usual, she'd made a ton of food for easy heat and serve, which she didn't have to do. It wasn't like we couldn't slap together a sandwich or order pizza, but she was one of the most nurturing people I'd ever known. Nothing like what our mom had been. Guilt sucker punched me at the thought, no matter how true it was.

I got comfortable on the island when the toast and coffee were ready. I munched away and waited for the fireworks to start. Damon came barreling down the stairs.

"What the hell, man?" He skidded through a particularly thick patch of Solo cups and spilled beer on the ruined wood floor. It would need to be cleaned, buffed, and restained. "Why didn't you get the cleaning service in here?"

A cruel smile pulled at my lips. "The evidence needed to remain. Just until Dad comes home." I glanced at my watch. "They'll be here soon."

Damon shook his head. "I don't even want to know." He grabbed his bag from the mud room, shouting at me as he headed for the garage. "I'll see you at practice."

The underlying scent of stale beer didn't deter me from enjoying my coffee. Twenty minutes later, I heard Riley moving around in her room. Perfect. She would be down soon, and my dad was due home any minute. I couldn't have timed it better if I'd tried.

I felt like a symphony conductor and clamped down on the laughter that wanted to break free as Riley came down the stairs at the exact moment my dad walked into the kitchen. His eyes bulged, and red infused his cheeks over his five-o'clock shadow of a beard.

"What the hell happened here, Cole?" Dad bellowed.

I took a sip of my coffee, thumbing over my shoulder to the hallway where Riley had to be, since I heard her on the stairs. "Looks like your woman's daughter likes to throw parties when her mom is out of town." It helped that we hadn't been caught with evidence of throwing them in years.

Dad stood there, his hands fisting at his sides, looking around the kitchen and living room in bewilderment before he pierced me with his lawyer stare. "Is that the story you're sticking to?"

I could feel his eyes bore into the side of my head with the heat of a thousand suns, but I wasn't giving in. "If it were me, you know I would have had a cleaning service here before you came home." I waved toward the floor. "This isn't my style."

Another minute passed with Dad rooted where he'd stopped at the entrance to the kitchen, dressed in his charcoal-gray suit.

"Did you drop Raelyn off somewhere?" I glanced toward the way he'd come in. "She's not with you?" Like I gave a shit. All the better to cause conflict between them, any of them.

"What the fuck," Dad muttered under his breath then stormed out of the room.

I got up from the island and deposited my dishes in the dishwasher before leaning against the entrance to the hall. Out of sight of Dad, I watched confusion flicker over Riley's face as he confronted her.

"I understand that you're new to the rules of the house, Riley. And we'll sit down when your mother returns from getting her hair done and go over them. But make no mistake that throwing an unapproved party and leaving a mess like this is unacceptable."

I could hear the fury, which he tried to mask, vibrating in his voice. Usually, he was more collected. This morning had caught him off guard. Riley met Dad's gaze without flinching. She didn't say a single thing to defend herself, which was exactly the wrong move. But she did catch my eye when he shifted to the side, and I took note of the violence simmering there. Good. I looked forward to our next encounter.

I gave her a little wave. She scowled before shifting her gaze back to Dad, holding her ground and refusing to say anything as his lecture continued. When he was done and stalking toward his study, I pivoted and headed out the door to practice, laughing as I got in my car. I couldn't wait to see how her mother reacted to the news.

CHAPTER TWENTY-FIVE

RILEY

Could this day get any worse? I'd checked my phone first thing and noticed all traces of my stealth video were gone. The minute I could escape the house, I would—but only after doing a little recon. Lucas was in his study. A cleaning service had shown up and was working hard on the mess Cole had made and blamed me for.

Checkmate, motherfucker. Anger was a volcano inside me. I would get him back.

After he and Damon were at football practice, I decided to do a little scouting in his room. I cracked open the door and peered down the hall. When I was sure the coast was clear, I tiptoed to his too-close-to-my-own room. I wasn't even sure where Mom was staying—maybe this was the kids' wing.

With my heart racing, I gripped the knob, gave it a slow turn, and pushed. I couldn't believe he hadn't locked his door. Stupid... although mine didn't have one either. I needed to address that.

Shock held me prisoner on the threshold for a second before I came to my senses and stepped fully inside. I shut the door behind me. The room was clean and orderly, not at all what I expected. I could have bet money that he and Damon lived like slobs with dirty clothes and dishes strewn about the room and the stench so foul I wouldn't have been able to remain there long. The only messy thing going on in Cole's room was the unmade bed.

It smelled like him. I took a moment to breathe in his addictive wild-spice-and-ocean scent. His room was decorated in dark gray and blue with accents of white. Combined with his scent, my overactive imagination pictured him lying shirtless on his bed, hands behind his head, his green eyes smoldering with desire, beckoning me to him. Shaking myself free of the mirage, I turned to his dresser and the framed pictures on the surface. Trailing a finger over the dark, dark wood, I stopped at a stunning brunette wearing a breathtaking smile. Two cute little boys were in her arms, struggling and laughing in an attempt to break free from her hug. My heart hurt just looking at the vibrant emotion from the black-and-white photo. That must have been his mom. I wonder what happened to her. Divorce, most likely.

Moving on, I opened various drawers and riffled through them. There wasn't much that could give me an advantage—no compromising pictures, no hidden drugs. The framed photos on the walls were of football: artistic shots of the field, the ball in motion, dramatic shots of goalposts.

The only constants here were football and order or perhaps control, based on the cleanliness and organization of his room.

That was what I would take away—control.

I opened a few more doors until I found Damon's room. There was no way I was going in there. It was as I'd expected, an utter explosion of dirty clothes. Luckily, no dishes. He wasn't my target, so I didn't waste time going through his disgusting mess.

Anger continued to churn as I snuck out of the house without Lucas seeing me. Once in my car, I pointed it toward the school. I needed to check out football practice. That asshole was doing more than stirring up trouble for me with Lucas and the bitch squad. He was trying to mess with my relationship with my mom by blaming the party's carnage on me.

It wouldn't work.

I hope. A tiny part of me worried because Mom had never gone full-on Stepford outside of a con and without involving me. The drive to school didn't take long, and when I got there, I parked by the football field. A couple of hours had already passed since Cole left, and I shouldn't have been surprised that the players weren't on the field anymore. Still, some sense propelled me forward, and as I passed through the opening to the stadium, I spotted a decent portion of the team finishing stretches or hanging around and talking.

I swear testosterone had a smell—sweat and body odor, mostly—and there was too much of it here. Not even a handful of steps into the stadium, I spotted him sitting in the bleachers, surrounded by several players, his brother and cousins, and a few of the bitch squad.

A wave of laughter spiked, and I was the center of their attention. *That fucker.* I narrowed my eyes at him, my cheeks heating as he met my gaze and smirked. Then he made a crude gesture to more laughter, and I froze, my blood running cold. I could only guess that he was telling them about what had happened between us last night, making a joke of it.

Screw him. I spun on my heel and stormed back to my car, hating how badly I wanted to hide. A new level of anger sizzled through me. I never ran from things. He had ruined so much already, and he didn't seem to be even remotely finished.

Throwing myself behind the wheel of my car, I put it in gear and tore out of the parking lot and back to the mansion. My eyes burned, but I refused to cry—another thing he'd almost brought me to the brink of.

I never cried. I hated him so much for everything he was putting me through.

Back at the house, the cleaning crew was hard at work, setting the house back to what it was before Cole's stupid party. And lucky for me, Lucas was nowhere in sight—*but where the hell is my mom?*

COLE

It pissed me off that Riley was here and even more that she left. The timing had been good. In the middle of telling a joke, I added something I knew she would misinterpret. Piper had her claws embedded in my arm for the little show, but with Riley gone, I sent her away then got up. Most of the players were in the locker room. The only ones remaining were a few of the defensive players who'd congregated on the track, my brother, and our cousins.

"Did you call a service to clean up the mess?" Damon leaned back on his elbows, studying me.

"Yeah, they should be close to done when we get home."

"Don't you think you're being a little hard on her?" Shane asked.

The only one with a girlfriend, he was softer around the edges regarding women. Not the rest of us. Phoenix loved his mom, but his anger over his dad overshadowed everything. He'd seen more than Shane had, the whole nightmare we endured with our mom and his aunt. I speared him with a look containing all the fury I felt with her and Raelyn living in my house after what they had done. "No."

The need for violence was too close to the surface, and rather than take it out on my cousin, I stood then descended the bleachers. To make things worse, every moment I'd spent with Riley in that bed tormented me. I wanted her—the enemy— badly. It was all-consuming, something I would have to satisfy and get out of my system before I sent her packing.

"Hey, Cole."

Bryce, a defensive guard, stopped me as I stepped off the bleachers. He was a solid guy and did a pretty good job in his position. My patience was hair-trigger at the moment as I walked to the locker rooms. He kept pace. "What?"

"Great party last night."

In ground-eating strides, I ignored him, almost at the doors that would lead to me taking a shower and getting the hell out of there.

"There was a girl there, one I haven't seen at our school before."

That got my attention, and I stopped, slowly pivoting until we were eye to eye, hoping like hell he would drop it. Because I had a feeling I knew who he was talking about, and Riley was mine. "What about her?"

"She's hot as hell. I saw her at the pool then talking to you last night. I don't want to step on your toes, but if you're done with her, I want to hit that."

Something snapped inside of me, all the rage I'd been holding in erupted, and I slammed my fist into his face. Through a red haze, time blinked out as I pounded on him. I wound back for another, but arms wrapped around me, pulling me away. With a roar, I struggled, wanting to go after him again.

"Cole!"

"Stop!"

Phoenix and my brother's shouts cut through the haze enough for me to see what I'd done to Bryce. Good. His left eye was swollen shut, and blood trickled down his split lip. Seeing him pissed me off all over again. "Do not touch her."

I'd yelled it, and I didn't give a shit who heard. The message had to be delivered.

Every inch of her was mine, and I would do the same or worse if any asshole thought he could have a taste. A few other defensive linemen herded Bryce into the locker room, casting shocked and wary glances at me.

Damon whirled on me when they were gone, leaving just my cousins and brother. "What the fuck is wrong with you?"

"You're getting in too deep," Phoenix warned, but his eyes were mercurial, and I knew he was close to jumping into a brawl beside me.

I couldn't control what raged inside me, so I said nothing. Shane was silent, but Damon wasn't finished.

"You need to figure out what's going on and get that girl out of your system. Last night was supposed to have different results." He punctuated that with a jab to my chest. "Get this shit handled."

I shoved away from them. I needed some distance. The rage was too close to the surface, and I had to calm down. I couldn't believe that they didn't understand what Riley and her mother signified. Mostly, it was my fault. I hadn't told them. Damon hadn't seen Raelyn that day at the conference. I would tell them soon, once I got Riley out of my head for good.

And the only way that was happening was to get in her pants and out of my fucking mind.

CHAPTER TWENTY-SEVEN

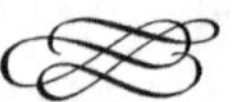

RILEY

Cole's under my skin. In my dreams. Everywhere I look.

The kiss was as intoxicating as the last. Better. And I hated him for it. Everything was wrong, reversed—he was the puppet master in our war. I didn't like it one bit.

I couldn't stay in the house, and after texting Cassie, I left and met her at a cute café. We sat on the patio at a four-top amidst dwarf palms and greenery that provided a natural, private ambiance. If only my mood had fit the luxurious environment. I was out of place, and distress radiated off me. It wasn't a good look or vibe.

Cass shoved a handful of sleek brown hair back then took another bite of her salad. I pushed mine around with my fork, not at all hungry. We'd chatted about mundane stuff, but I knew it was time to confess when she gave me that no-bullshit steady stare.

That was why I'd wanted to get together in the first place. Dishing to a friend didn't come easily to me. It'd always been just Mom and me. I had to say, it was pretty cool to have someone to talk to. If we stayed here for the year as Mom promised, I could keep my only friend.

"Okay. Enough." Cass's fork clattered against the wide, shallow bowl. "I didn't go to the party last night, since I was on babysitting duty with my sister, so I don't know what happened. Obviously, something did. Spill."

I put my fork down, too, giving up all pretense that I would eat anything. "I went but not by choice."

Her light brows furrowed. "Explain."

"I didn't get a chance to tell you because it happened so fast." I caught the ends of my hair and tugged on them nervously. "My mom and I moved into Lucas Savage's house. That's who she's dating—engaged to."

"What?" Her mouth hung open for a few seconds. "Your mom is engaged to Cole and Damon's dad? And you're living there? I'm sorry, this is what you tell your best friend?" She motioned between us. "Because that's what we are."

Warmth chased some of the anxiety from my body, and I grinned. "Best friends, huh?"

She rolled her eyes. "Yeah, obviously. Now, get to the good stuff. What happened?"

I took a deep breath then filled her in on everything. The surprising move into his house. The threats, the party, the kiss, and that we'd done a little more too. Just thinking about it sent a wave of heat up my neck to settle uncomfortably on my cheeks.

"Back up." Her fingers curled around the edge of the table. "He kissed you, and what? Was it amazing? You're dating... I don't understand what's going on."

"This is where it gets fucked up. The kiss. I've never been kissed like that before. You weren't kidding about the Elite. They're different. I can't get how he made me feel out of my head, and believe me, I've tried because he's a major asshole. Even though I want him, I hate him. I just hope I hate him enough to resist him if it happens again."

She waved her hand around. "Why? I must be missing something here. You guys made out and did a little... extra. So things should be good, right?" I scowled, and her eyes went wide. "What did the bastard do?"

I shrugged. "It was… weird. I mean, he kissed me with so much heat and passion. Same with the way he touched me. Then after, he got up, and it was like a wall slammed over his face. He was so cold. Dismissive. And the asshole left my room with the door open. I was half-naked!"

"That bastard. I'm going to murder him." Cass slammed her hands on the table, rattling the dishes.

I grabbed her glass before it spilled then gripped her forearms, keeping her focused on me. "I just want to forget about it. Which is probably easier said than done, given how much I liked it when he touched me."

"Pff. That's an easy fix. We just need to find you someone to hook up with. Then you won't need that asshole."

"That's not a bad idea." I relaxed back into my chair, my appetite slowly returning. It seemed like we would be here a while because of Mom's engagement. "Huh, I might be able to go on a real date." That traitorous part of me automatically thought of Cole. *Bad idea.* Anything with him would only bring trouble—he was determined to ruin me.

Cass mimicked me by leaning back in her chair too. "I've seen a few of the football players eyeing you. That's a good place to start."

I didn't care. So long as it was anyone other than Cole. "Enough about me. Tell me what happened this weekend with Matt. You guys went surfing yesterday, right?"

A smile curved Cass's lips, and her eyes grew dreamy and unfocused. "It was magical. We surfed. Hung out. And I've decided I want to have his little surfer babies."

I tossed a crouton at her. "You're crazy. Did he kiss you?"

"Yeah," she sighed. "It was so hot. Then my mom opened the door and ruined everything. Story of my life." She lobbed the crouton back.

I grinned. "That had to be awkward. Are you going out again?"

She shrugged, and some of the excitement faded. "I don't know. He didn't say anything. I hate this part. The waiting to see if he likes me as much as I do him."

"He would be crazy not to want to go out with you."

Carefree laughter fell from her mouth, bringing with it a return of happiness. "You're right, of course."

My phone pinged, and I glanced at it then did a double take. "Um, my mom is texting— yelling, actually, for me to get my butt home."

"Home, huh?" Cass winked.

I caught the waiter's attention so we could pay our bill. "Not in this lifetime."

CHAPTER TWENTY-EIGHT

COLE

The walls closed in. Back and forth, I paced in my room. Practice hadn't helped. Nothing did—Riley was in my fucking head.

She wasn't home. I'd checked. One good thing. Right?

I wasn't entirely sure.

Our attraction was insane, nothing like I'd experienced before. I had no problem messing around or sleeping with a girl then putting her from my mind. But Riley was different. I was obsessed with her, which was a problem because she had to go. She and her mother.

I'd done what research I could. Something about them didn't add up. There was nothing to find, no pictures or social media accounts. What seventeen-year-old didn't have social media? It was a huge red flag that they weren't who they claimed to be.

It was time to enlist help. I punched in the number of the private investigator Dad had used on more than one occasion. He was the best, and if anyone could uncover what they were hiding, it would be him. I continued to pace while waiting for him to answer.

"Westman Private Investigations."

I stopped at the sound of the gruff voice, resting a hip against my desk. "Wes, this is Cole Savage."

"Cole. What's going on? Are you working for your dad now?"

"No." It made sense that he would think I was calling to get Wes on one of Dad's cases. "I need to hire you to look into two people. Not for Dad."

I was eighteen, so there was no question about legalities, as if that mattered to Wes. After filling him in on the little I'd learned about Raelyn and Riley Matthews, we ended the call with him saying, "It'll take a bit."

I didn't want to play around with time. The sooner I had information on them, the better. Their presence in my house would only cause further problems for Damon, Dad, and me. Especially since I'd caught Damon talking to Raelyn at lunch the other day. He hadn't seemed as angry, but he would be when he found out who she really was. I didn't want it to get to the point that he developed a relationship with either of them, which was unlikely but a chance I wasn't willing to take.

I pulled up the picture I'd taken of Raelyn's driver's license. I'd gotten it from her wallet. Unable to sit around and wait for news, I decided to check out the address listed there. It was in the same town but in an area everyone knew was dangerous. If that was where they came from, they were definitely using my father for his money. Not that I blamed them. Dad was an asshole and deserved it.

Decision made, I grabbed my phone, punched the address into my GPS, and got on the road. The drive would help. I could calm down and try to figure out why Riley affected me so much. It wasn't that she was gorgeous. She was, but it was something else. The chemistry between us was unusual and unique, and I felt in my gut that it was a once-in-a-lifetime thing. But that couldn't have been correct. She wasn't for me, just as Raelyn would not be in my father's life when I got through with them.

When I finally got there, I discovered run-down duplexes lining the street. I'd done enough digging to know that they were rentals. The lack of care was evident in the cracked steps, broken railings, and paint peeling around the trim of the buildings. The windows weren't much better. The bottom ones had bars on them, and a majority looked as if they hadn't been washed in years.

Two women were smoking on the steps. I bet they were there often. I smiled and walked up, ensuring there was enough distance between us that they didn't feel intimidated. Violent crimes happened there on the regular. "Hey, ladies. I wonder if you can help me with some information."

"What's a pretty boy like you doing here?" The larger one snickered then took a deep drag on her cigarette. A cloud of smoke was blown in my direction.

"Do you know who lives in this house?" I pointed with my thumb over my shoulder. "Past tenants? Or do I need to contact the landlord for that information?" Better to let them know they weren't the only option to get the info I wanted.

"No need for that," the rail-thin woman with sparse mousy brown hair rasped. "We've lived here for the past ten years and know everything. Same guy owns that house, this one, and five others on this block. The landlord is a joke. Collects the rent and doesn't fix shit."

"I know the type." Not entirely true, but I understood people.

"You a cop?" The larger woman who liked to blow smoke at me squinted.

"No. But I'm looking for information about Raelyn and Riley Matthews. Did you know them?"

"Them two are popular. The last man who came looking for them paid for his answers."

Fine, whatever. I took out my wallet and handed each a twenty-dollar bill. "Did either of you know them?"

"Yes," the smoker replied then fanned herself with the bill.

Fuck. This was going to cost me. I took out another twenty each but waited to give it to them. "What can you tell me about them? Something useful."

"Not much to tell, but triple that, and we'll share what we know," the skinny one bartered.

"This is it." I got the money from my wallet. "If you don't give me something worthwhile, I'll go door to door, asking people while waiting for the landlord to show."

They nodded, and I gave them the money.

"They were all right," Skinny answered. "Kept to themselves but could also handle themselves."

"What do you mean by that?" I didn't like the thought of Riley needing to know how to fight. Is that what she was talking about?

"It's just an observation," Smoker said. "Living here, you know who not to mess with. They were pretty on the outside, and I knew people tried, but"—she tapped the corner of her eye with her index finger—"it was the eyes that told us not to even bother messing with them."

"And we heard things." Skinny shrugged. "They weren't here all that long. A few weeks, tops. Paid rent in cash. Not sure what they did for a living. The kid went out some days. Some days, she didn't. The mom didn't keep regular hours either."

"Who else was looking for them?"

Smoker clammed up, her answer clipped. "Big guy. Mean. Don't know his name."

It was clear our time was almost done. I asked a few more questions but didn't get anything useful. Back in the car, I headed home, more confused than ever. I called the PI and relayed what I'd found out. I guessed he would visit the landlord and a few tenants, but I wasn't sure he'd learn anything more than I had.

Even though what I'd learned was good, it wasn't enough to convince my father or use it to blackmail Raelyn into breaking his heart.

CHAPTER TWENTY-NINE

RILEY

Rebellion wasn't my jam. Acting out wasn't either. Why would I behave like a typical teenager? I wasn't one. Mom texted. I came home. Simple.

Only it wasn't.

This was total bullshit. She was upset about something I hadn't even done. Did she not know me? It sure as hell felt like I didn't know her anymore.

I was in the McMansion, as she'd requested, but in my room. I didn't look for her when I got back. She could find me. Whatever argument was brewing, I wasn't on board with it. There was one saving grace: I didn't think Cole and Damon were home.

Watching videos on my phone, I didn't bother to look up when my door burst open. It was either Mom or Cole. Why spoil the surprise? I waited. It wasn't long to find out it was Mom, and she got right to the point.

Her hands planted on her hips as she glared. "What were you possibly thinking, throwing a party?"

Seriously? Hurt and anger rolled through me, and I met her stormy gaze with my own, tossing my phone on the bed beside me. "I can't believe you. It wasn't my fault."

"This is ridiculous." She dug in her pocket, pulled her phone out and clicked on something, then turned it to me. "I found this posted online. I had to call your uncle to get it taken down. You better hope he wiped it before people we can't have seeing it did."

Oh shit. I grabbed her phone and stared at a picture Cole had taken at the party. I didn't quite register him taking it, nor had I thought he would post it. And with my bedhead and heavy-lidded eyes, I looked drunk.

"That's not what you think it was." *Since when does Mom not take my word over all others'?* I was steadily hating on our newly messed-up relationship. *Fucking Lucas. What type of brainwashing has he done?* "Besides, he hasn't seen me in years and doesn't know what I look like now."

Mom pressed her lips together so tightly that they were white. Her chin came up, and crap, I recognized the look. It was the one that meant there was no getting through to her. I'd had the misfortune of encountering her stubborn, unreasonable side twice before. Those weren't great memories, but we always worked through whatever had set her off. Usually fear. *So what is she so afraid of? Losing her fiancé?* My head thumped against the headboard, and I fought against doing it repeatedly.

"Yes, Riley, he does, because this is what I looked like at your age."

"Then let's leave." But I knew it was already too late to sway her to my way of thinking. She was too far gone into the fear and would probably say things she didn't mean. I didn't fully understand, but deep down, I got it. After all, I'd seen her the one time he'd caught up with us when I was little.

"You've hated Cole since the day we moved here." Mom's eyes were wild. "Why are you trying to get him in trouble?"

It was like a slap in the face, and I clamped my mouth shut.

Anything I said would only fuel her or cause me to say that she was acting like a bitch. I inhaled through my nose to try to calm down a little. We were usually on the same page, but we hadn't been since we moved to this stupid town. "Why would I throw a party like that?"

"Because you're angry about the engagement and want to get us thrown out." She practically vibrated with fury, and her eyes took on that crazy look like she'd had the time we fled that duplex dump last summer, which had also been in California.

It made me think that our past had caught up with us or that what she wanted wouldn't work out. What that was, I hadn't gotten a chance to find out. She hadn't completed the last con here, so we'd fled in the middle of the night after a call from my uncle. *Does what's happening now have anything to do with what happened last year?*

Mom crossed her arms over her chest. "Do you want to go back to cons and running?"

Sort of. But then I thought of the possibility of staying the year, of having a friend, of the diving team. I'd never been able to be on one before for fear of pictures, media. We couldn't draw attention. "Screw you." I'd had enough. "I didn't do anything wrong."

"I don't want to hear it, Riley."

"And I could give a shit about your stupid engagement"—I had to get a dig in, because fuck her—"if it's even real."

"I'm calling your uncle. It's clear that you need a reminder of the kind of life we might have to go back to if you keep acting out."

***

The start of the school week was brutal without caffeine, and I regretted sleeping in as I moved through the halls and sat in classes to snide looks and comments. It wasn't something I was used to dealing with, since I was usually a chameleon, fitting in but never drawing attention to myself. This was some next-level bullshit.

I shoved my calculus book in my locker, exchanging it for physics—the last class of this worthless day.

Cassie's shoulder hit the locker next to mine, her lips curving in a half-hearted smile. "How are you doing?"

I slammed my locker door shut and rolled my eyes at the word Slut written across it. "Eh, I'll survive."

Her gaze fixed over my shoulder and hardened. "I'm going to talk to Damon. Things are getting out of hand."

"No." God, that was the last thing I needed. Not that he would fight my battle, but this juvenile prank was a girl thing. "I have to put an end to this."

"You may have your chance, then." She gave a nod to what she was tracking. "Bitch squad walking your way." She squeezed my arm. "I've got your back."

"Appreciate it, but let me handle them. Meet me in class?"

She frowned, looking toward the girls who were almost upon us. "I—"

"Please. Go." After passing Cass my book so both hands were free and she reluctantly left, I turned then leaned against my locker. Piper, Teagan, Tracey, and Jessica were making a direct path through the students to me. But I was ready. I might have to keep to the background, but since Mom swore this place was different, I was going to take a bitch down.

They stopped in a half circle, surrounding me. My hands were loose. I was ready for anything. In any of the other schools, I would have been about to get into a knock-down, drag-out fight. Here, I kind of doubted it, even though I wanted to smear her plastic face all over the locker behind me.

"Slut."

"Original." I grinned, enjoying this more than I thought I

would. "Did you come up with that yourself, Malibu Barbie? Or did you have help from your minions?"

Piper sneered, and her entourage closed ranks, so there was no getting out unless I pushed them out of my way, which I wasn't opposed to doing.

"This is just the beginning, bitch," Tracey sneered. "The Elite are out of reach for trailer trash like you."

"Well, they are tall. Is that the message you're attempting to deliver?" I'd seen Tracey hanging all over Shane more often than not in school. "I'm guessing that's why you're wearing hooker heels. Ambitious."

"As amusing as this is," Piper said, resuming control of her minions with a side glance at Tracey, "it's in poor taste to try to sleep with your stepbrother. I'm here to spell it out for you if his rejection at the party didn't make sense. Cole is mine. Back off, slut."

I laughed under my breath as they filed away. They wanted to fight with insults, with words. There wouldn't be anything physical—yet. I wanted to push for an actual fight. I had all kinds of pent-up discontent and rage from the rift between Mom and me, the bullshit with Cole, and my pending discussion with Uncle Ronan.

Those bitches didn't know who they were messing with.

CHAPTER THIRTY

RILEY

I tossed and turned, the covers tangling around my legs like ropes. I kicked one free before sinking into sleep. But it didn't last long. My mind raced even in my dreams, bringing me to the heart of what plagued me.

Something's wrong. I knew it in my bones. Mom and I had a connection that stemmed from a greater place than uncondi-tional love—it came from survival. And my gut was screaming that I needed to do something.

She should have been home two hours ago, and I would have gotten a text if she was running late. But nada. I pulled up the app to find her phone, raced out of the dump we were staying in, and followed the directions that would lead me to where she was.

I didn't recognize the address, but it wasn't far. I checked the map. I had seven blocks to go before turning left. We were in Hoboken, close to the river, and cars whizzed past on the busy street. I dodged pedestrians that didn't pay me the slightest bit of attention. They shouldn't. I blended into a crowd even at thirteen with my choice of clothes and lack of eye contact. None of it was new to me.

Mom hadn't wanted to stay here too long, but we both decided one extra day would be okay. I was terrified that we'd made a huge mistake.

I swiped the screen and found Uncle Ronan's contact. Not bothering to text, I hit the button to call him. He answered immediately.

"Mom's not home." I didn't need to say more. He knew I wouldn't call about her being late unless it was an emergency.

I heard a door close on his end of the line then a car engine rev. "I see her location. Do not go there, Riles."

I hung up. Too late.

He could track both Mom and me with each new phone number by downloading the app the three of us shared. We'd made a deal a long time ago. And it could save Mom's life if she was in the kind of trouble my gut said she was.

I broke into a run, uncaring if I drew attention. Three blocks, and I would be where her phone was. *Please be there. Alive.*

When I got to where the map showed me her phone was, I stood in front of an expensive-looking hotel. My eyes misted. There had to be about fifteen floors; all I could tell was that she was in the back left corner. I would have to go floor by floor, checking that general area. *I can do this.*

My baseball hat shielded part of my face. The sunglasses helped too. I tucked my hair into my oversized hoodie, bunching the hood to hide where it flowed from my hat. If who I suspected had Mom, they would check the cameras after Uncle Ronan and I broke her out. I had to stay well hidden. Mom had worked too hard for me to blow my identity now.

I went through a brass turnstile and into a lobby with marble floors, high ornate ceilings dripping with chandeliers, and oil paintings adorning the walls. Soft music flowed through hidden speakers. Large plants surrounded small gathering areas for hotel guests. People came and went. I could blend.

I avoided the lobby's reception desk and hit the halls, looking for the first maid I could find. I didn't run into any until the second floor. I spotted one with the door to the room she was cleaning propped open while she rummaged through her cart. She turned enough so I could see the front of her uniform, which didn't hold a clip for the card that would open any of the rooms. Her wrists didn't have the keycard tethered, so it had to be in one of her pockets. Closer, I paid attention to her dominant hand. It was her right. I would have to search her right pocket.

Increasing my pace, I lightly brushed against her, slipping my fingers into the front pocket of her uniform simultaneously. Tucking the piece of plastic into my palm and then pocket, I raised my other hand in a wave without looking behind me. "Sorry."

At the end of the hall, I grabbed the door for the stairwell and yanked it open. I needed to go back to the first floor and check the room. I raced down the stairs, my heart kicking into overdrive and nerves making me go even faster.

My palms slammed into the bar to open the steel door. I burst through and into the hallway. Not my most brilliant move. Luckily, there wasn't anyone around. My hands shook as I tried the first door on my left. It took a few tries until I got the keycard in and a green light to show. I rapped my knuckles on the door and said, "Housekeeping."

There was no response to the first two, and the rooms were empty when I opened the doors. I moved onto the third door as a familiar face appeared from the end of the hall. I almost sagged in relief. The dark-brown hair and eyes that looked so much like mine and Mom's belonged to Uncle Ronan. He was large and broad and promised pain to anyone who messed with us. I didn't like the fury on his face from seeing me here, but I would deal with that later. I slid the card into the next door and heard the rumble of deep voices when I cracked open the door.

This could go either way. I pushed open the door, murmuring "housekeeping" as I had before. Two men stood near the end of the bed. That wasn't what caused bile to climb my throat. It was the figure crumbled on the bloodied duvet that did. "Mom!"

I rushed into the room as the first goon reached for me. Uncle Ronan crashed inside, and a muffled sound pierced the buzzing in my ear. Blood splattered the side of my face. I ignored it and rushed to where she lay. Tears streamed down my cheeks.

Blood caked her swollen and cracked lips. One eye was swollen shut. Both were closed. A trail of blood ran from the corner of her mouth into a small puddle on the white blanket. There was a quarter-sized lump on the right side of her forehead, and tears stained the front of her cream-colored shirt. But what scared me the most were the red, angry marks wringing her slender neck, telling of the large hands that had squeezed until she couldn't breathe.

I vaguely heard the scuffle of men and the thump of someone's fist slamming into flesh. I had every faith that my uncle would handle the situation. My only concern was that she was alive.

I didn't know where to touch. Gently, I pressed my fingers against her neck, checking for a pulse. Steady beating brought me to my knees, and I let out a sob of relief. But she was so broken. I hated him for doing this to her. Her ex. My father. If he'd taken her from me, I would have hunted him down and made him pay. Nothing would have stopped me.

"We've got to go," Uncle Roman growled as he moved to the other side of the bed and gathered Mom into his arms.

Then, I saw blood seeping into the carpet and two men lying dead in the middle of it. I jolted back and then met his eyes. "Why?" It was a stupid question. I knew why. And I wasn't sorry for what had happened to them.

"They saw you. There can't be any evidence."

The picture. My mind jolted from the horrific nightmare to the picture Cole had taken of me at the party—what had triggered it. *He's coming.*

I jerked awake with a gasp. It was dark. A hand pressed against my shoulder, and a large form leaned over me. I reacted without thinking and swung with everything I had in me. Blind panic consumed me, and I fought with desperation.

"Riley." He pinned my hands above, and his leg trapped mine. "Stop."

Cole's deep voice slowly penetrated as I bucked against his hold. *It's not him.*

Cole wasn't good, but he didn't want to hurt me. I sagged back against my pillow, and to my utter horror, tears leaked from my eyes. I shook uncontrollably from adrenaline and shock. I knew it, but there wasn't anything I could do to stop it. I tried to turn away when he released his hold on me, but he climbed onto the bed. A sob slipped free, and I buried my face in my hands and turned into him.

It was a moment of weakness. Everyone had them, right? This was mine.

He wrapped me in his embrace. One hand held my head to his chest, and the other rubbed soothing circles over my back. I fisted his T-shirt, shivering with fear. The image of Mom the day her ex had found her was burned into my mind. That careless picture that Cole had posted could do so much damage. I was such a fool.

Minutes passed. How many, I wasn't sure. All cried out, I lay in his arms, not wanting to move from the security he offered. When he went to shift, I tensed. "Don't." I was ashamed to need him, but God, I did.

"What was that about, Riley?"

I shook my head against his chest. "Just a nightmare. But..." I didn't want to say it.

"I'll stay. But you have to give me something. Was that a nightmare or a memory?"

"A nightmare." It was both. A partial truth.

"I don't believe you."

The deep cadence of his voice as it rumbled through his chest and into mine relaxed me further. I didn't have the energy to fight with him. He was complex and controlling, but a part of me trusted him. I wasn't going to question that.

"Truce for tonight?"

He understood. I released against him, my eyelids drifting shut. "We can go back to hating each other tomorrow."

He chuckled into my hair. *He can fight.* It was in the back of my mind. And while we had shared animosity, there was also want and need.

Will he help me if things go to hell?

When morning came, Cole was gone. Did I want that? *Yes!*

School dragged. Between the nightmare and confusion over Cole's behavior, I felt like a zombie walking the halls. Not the best-case scenario when the Barbie Club was around every corner.

One more class and then lunch. That and lit class were the only hours I looked forward to because I shared them with Cass. A shoulder hit me—big surprise. My body half turned from the impact, and I stumbled a little but recovered.

The bell was about to ring, so I hurried forward, not paying attention until something hard hit my ankle. My leg flew out from under me, and already in an awkward position, I couldn't recover. I cringed, bracing for impact as the floor rushed me.

A steel band wrapped around my waist and swooped me back to my feet. It happened so fast that I was dizzy. Blinking the world back into focus, I turned to my rescuer then sucked in a breath. Cole's green eyes blazed furiously, but he didn't direct them at me. I followed his line of sight to Piper, who had a fake smile on her face.

"What the fuck, Piper?" Cole growled.

I was still mute. *What is happening?*

"What?" She shrugged a slender shoulder. "She's clumsy." With a flick of her hair, she disappeared into class.

Cole dropped his arm, and I moved aside to put some distance between us. "Thanks," I murmured then rounded the corner as Damon converged on his brother. Something made me pause, just out of sight in the next hallway.

"So now you're saving her?" Amusement colored Damon's voice.

"I want her frozen out, not injured." Cole snapped.

Huh. I hurried into my classroom so they didn't catch me, but I was glad I'd stayed to listen.

I had a hard time believing it and wouldn't if that hadn't happened. But... maybe Cole wasn't the complete asshole that I thought?

CHAPTER THIRTY-ONE

COLE

Football practice was done, and Damon was out with some girl he'd been eyeing in the bleachers. It was the middle of the week, and Dad had texted that he and Raelyn were in the city for a client dinner. The only person who would be home was Riley.

Her car was in the driveway. I prowled through the house, checking her room and every other one. I found a shoe of hers. A discarded hair tie. Even a T-shirt. I collected them all, depositing them in my room for her to have to get.

She wasn't anywhere.

Things had been escalating with the girls bullying her. A normal girl would have crumbled. So far, she hadn't. If anything, she seemed amused. I couldn't figure her out, and it was driving me crazy.

Hungry, I grabbed the handle to open the fridge to take out whatever Louisa had left for dinner when I heard muffled voices coming from the patio. Good thing I hadn't opened it yet or turned on any lights. *Who is she talking to?* It had better not be Damon. He'd softened toward her because she hadn't ratted us out about the party, and I didn't like it. Hurrying to the door that led outside from the living room, I cracked it open enough to slip out to the lanai and into the shadows.

From my position, I had a good view of Riley and a man I'd never seen before. He was large, about my height, six-two. He hugged her. I didn't recognize him, but how she responded told me she was familiar with him. *Who is he? Her father?* Their voices were faint, and I inched closer so I could hear.

"You didn't have to come here, Uncle Ronan," Riley said.

An uncle. It might not be enough to do anything with, but I had a first name. I wished there was some light so I could see his face.

"Raelyn called. Whatever's going on with you, it was enough to have her circle the wagons. I'm here. Spill."

I recognized his voice when he spoke. It was the same guy Raelyn had been talking to the other night. And while his being her uncle decreased a small portion of my suspicion, talking in private and behind Dad's back was still suspect.

"I don't know. Things are so fucked up. Mom isn't acting normal. I mean, she didn't believe me about the party. When has something like that ever happened? We have a great relationship, but lately..."

"She's all about the new guy?" Ronan's deep voice was harder to hear. "Shutting you out? Treating you like she's your mom instead of a sister or best friend?"

"That's exactly how it is, and I hate it."

He chuckled. "She's still all those things, but the mom side, the one who's hoping for a different life for both of you... that's what's coming out, Riles."

"I'm almost eighteen. I don't need her to shut me out and try to be a parent like one of these overprivileged kids have. I just want her, what we've always been. I don't know. I'm—"

"Give her a little time. She'll get her head out of her ass. I know my sister. She thinks she's protecting you and trying to set you up for a life neither of you've had for the past seventeen years."

"And if she's wrong? What will her fiancé do when he discovers the truth about how we've survived all these years?"

Bingo. That was what I needed to hear. Whatever she and Raelyn were hiding wasn't going to stay that way for long. I would find out everything.

Ronan and Riley talked for a little while longer but not about anything I could use. I waited, silently melding into the shadows, until he left. Riley stayed on the patio couch, her head against the cushions as she looked at the sky. There weren't any stars out tonight with the cloud cover and call for rain. Dampness hung in the air, and a humid breeze told of the pending shower.

After I was sure Ronan was gone, I slipped through the lanai door then threw myself on the couch next to Riley. Her head whipped toward me, and I could make out the whites of her eyes with how big they were. I'd surprised her. Good.

"What the hell?" Her voice rose with each word. "Were you lurking around in the bushes, watching us?"

"Not quite. I happened to be on the lanai. Imagine my surprise when I overheard you meeting with your uncle. So tell me, what secret past were you talking about there?"

"None of your business." Her voice was stiff, clipped.

I'd caught her, and I think I rattled her for the first time.

"What do you have against Mom and me? I know there's more than the spoiled-brat persona you portray. Something deeper, darker. I can see it in your eyes. *So tell me,* why do you really want us gone?"

"That's not up for discussion." I needed to stay away from that line of questioning because all it did was make me angry. "What do you think my dad's going to think when he learns your uncle is here sneaking around?"

"That's not my problem." Bitterness coated her words, and I

remembered how upset she was about the way her mom was acting. "When Lucas finds out about him, she can deal with him. I don't care what your dad thinks."

For once, I felt we were on the same team, but the thought was a fleeting one.

"Nice job with the video. I'll be sure to save it to a few other locations next time."

She surprised me by bringing it up. "There won't be a next time, Riles." I used the nickname I heard her mom call her by. "You're in my world. The sooner you realize it, the better."

She pulled her knees up to her chest, wrapping her arms around them. "Why do you hate me so much?"

Her question took me by surprise, and I responded with honesty, not realizing how it would eventually shift the odds against me. "I don't hate you. I hate my father."

The End

No one, and I mean no one, had ever caught mom or me with my uncle. There was a reason for that—a very important one. And Cole had information on me that could be my ultimate downfall. Mom's too.

He has a name.

Continue reading the Hidden Valley Elite series with Savage Truth:
https://www.islavaughnauthor.com/books

Keep up with Isla's releases by joining her newsletter:
https://bit.ly/IslaVaughnNewsletter

If you enjoyed reading SAVAGE LIES as much as I did writing it, I hope you'll consider leaving a review.

ABOUT THE AUTHOR

Isla Vaughn is the author of the Hidden Valley Elite series. Her romance books are full of complex characters, strong alpha males, and the fierce women who bring them to their knees. When not writing, she can be found daydreaming about owning a beach house, reading, or drinking too much coffee.

You can find her at:
https://www.islavaughnauthor.com

Subscribe to Isla's newsletter for cover reveals, book announcements, and giveaways: https://bit.ly/IslaVaughnNewsletter

facebook.com/author.IslaVaughn
instagram.com/islavaughnauthor
tiktok.com/@islavaughnauthor
bookbub.com/profile/isla-vaughn
goodreads.com/islavaughn_author

ALSO BY ISLA VAUGHN

Hidden Valley Elite Series

Savage Start

Savage Lies

Savage Truth

Brutal Days

Brutal Nights

Cruel Start

Cruel Hate

Cruel Love

Wicked Games

Wicked Ends